Hush Little Baby

ALSO BY CAROLINE B. COONEY

Wanted!

The Terrorist

Flight #116 Is Down

Emergency Room

Twins

CAROLINE B.

COONEY

HUSH LITTLE BABY

SCHOLASTIC INC.

New York Toronto London Syndey Auckland

Mexico City New Delhi Hong Kong

ISBN 0-590-81974-7

12 11 10 9 8 7 6 1 2 3/0

Printed in the U.S.A. 01

First Scholastic printing, January 1999

For Ann Reit —
my first and my much-loved editor

Chapter 1

The day was very still. No cloud touched the blue sky. No garage door was open. No child was outdoors. No radio played. Automatic sprinklers had lifted and well-behaved water sprinkled neatly on green lawns.

Kit unlocked the front door of her father's vacant house and stood on the threshold like a stranger. This doorway was where she felt the divorce most intensely.

A few years ago, when Mom and Dad split and Mom remarried, it had been decided that Kit and Mom would move to New Jersey with Mom's new husband, Malcolm. There was little fighting between her parents about the decision to take Kit from her California roots and from Dad. Dad loved extravagant gestures, so he just bought a second house near Mom's new one, and commuted between New Jersey and California. The new houses were in Seven Hills, a spread-fingered development of dead-end roads circling a beautiful golf course.

The air inside Dad's house was stale, because Dad was in Los Angeles for two weeks, sometimes three. Dad and his partners created TV specials and he was always hunting down concepts and ideas. His second business involved sales to Japan and China, and his partner for that was in Seattle. But whenever he could, he'd fly in to Newark Airport, drive to Seven Hills, and live a quarter mile from Mom and Malcolm and Kit. This had been going on for two years, and they hadn't had too many major breakdowns. What with e-mail, fax, and overnight delivery, Dad could work anyplace, and he appeared to enjoy coast-to-coast living.

Shades and drapes were drawn, the rooms dark and silent. Kit shut off the alarms so she could leave the door open.

Dad had not brought a single thing from the California house in which Kit had grown up and which he'd kept after the divorce. He wanted the California house to be exactly the same for when Kit visited.

So when he bought the house in Seven Hills, he placed an order with a decorator, and slowly the decorator's choice of furniture and paintings, candlesticks and curtains filled the place. The decorator had a key, and whenever Kit came over there would be new pillows on the sofa, new avant-garde photographs carefully placed on a wall.

It was not a hotel, because the decorator had added so much stuff, and yet it was exactly like a hotel, because nothing in the house was Dad's or Kit's. Dad had maid service and yard service, and all he did was check in now and then, and the towels were sure to be clean and neatly folded.

Dusty had momentarily imposed her presence on the house: clothing, shoes, doll collection, and fashion magazines. But when Dusty left, there was no trace of her, just the way there was no trace of the people who had stayed at a hotel before you.

Kit had come to get a particular sweatshirt, and she had not walked from Mom and Malcolm's house using the sidewalks, but had followed the rough edges of the golf course. She loved the hummocks of tall grass, the hanging tree branches, and the need to watch out for golfers who couldn't hit straight. She'd skulk through the heavy shrubbery and for a minute or two she wouldn't be sixteen, but a little girl with secrets, vanishing to her hiding place.

When Kit heard a car coming down the short dead-end lane, she thought it was the mail carrier, a chubby, happy woman who gave Milk-Bones to dogs and lollipops to toddlers. No mail was delivered here, of course, but Mom and Malcolm got a vast quantity, being people who ordered from every catalog that ever arrived.

But the car that whipped into the driveway was no mail person.

It was Kit's ex-stepmother, Dusty.

The cul-de-sac was too short for a car to gather much speed, but Dusty had managed speed. Screeching up the driveway, Dusty lurched to a halt and then yanked the parking brake so hard the car bucked. Dusty was a poor driver, but she knew it and usually drove slowly to make up for it — so slowly that she was frequently rear-ended. Dusty's car was constantly in the shop being repaired. Probably that was why Kit didn't recognize this car; it was a loaner from the shop.

Dusty leaped out of her plain black sedan without glancing at the house, so she didn't see Kit. She tugged frantically at the door to the backseat, but it was locked. Whimpering with frustration, Dusty reached back inside the driver's door and over to the rear to release the lock. Then she pulled the door open, leaned way inside, and struggled to move something.

Dusty hadn't turned off the engine, but the car wasn't moving; for once she must have remembered to put it in park and set the brake. Over the peaceful hum of the engine, Kit could hear a little row of sobs, hiccups of distress.

Kit was very sorry she had chosen this particular moment to arrive at the house. She had plenty of sweatshirts at home. Forget the original plan. She would gently and swiftly close the door before Dusty saw her, and flit out the back so they would not cross paths.

Poor Dusty was well named. She did much better on the shelf than actually out there in the world trying to function. Considering the life Dad led — two coasts, two careers, two secretaries, two families — it was inconceivable that he would fall for a woman who could barely manage two phone calls. It wasn't long after his marriage to Dusty that Dad was just embarrassed, and wanted Dusty to go.

Dusty clung on, and only Kit was nice to her, because Kit felt awful for people who didn't have much brains.

Even now, fussing around in the backseat, unable to shift whatever she was after, Dusty was visibly confused. Finally she straightened up. She shifted her body in a hip to the left, hip to the right sort of way, and turned to face the house. She was bent over an enormous white plastic thing, hung with cloth.

"Kit!" cried Dusty. An expression of true delight crossed Dusty's face. She scurried up the brick walk, calling, "Kit! Kit! Kit!" Dusty liked repeating words. "Oh, Kit!" she cried. "Kit, this is so wonderful, you can help me, I had no idea you would be here, I thought the house would be empty!"

It was certainly supposed to be empty. Dad was in California, and he and Dusty were no longer married. Dusty no longer had possessions here and wasn't supposed to have a key. She wasn't the revenge type; this wasn't going to be an armload of dead roses. But what could Dusty be doing here?

Kit felt a sort of affection for Dusty.

Dusty looked terrible. Kit had never seen her anything other than beautifully dressed and coordinated. (If there was one thing Dusty did well, it was accessorize.) Usually her long, shiny gold hair curved along her shoulders, swinging and free. Now for the first time, Kit realized that Dusty dyed her hair, because the roots were dark and revolting. Dusty needed a shampoo, and her clothing did not fit and was wrinkled.

Dusty? For whom fashion and makeup were the two major reasons to be alive?

"Oh, Dusty!" she said. "What's wrong? Come on in. I'll get you something cold to drink." Whatever this was, Kit would have to solve it. Dad wanted no part of Dusty's pathetic problems, because they were always rooted in stupid decisions. Anyway, he was in California. Mom and Malcolm might be nearby, but nothing was going to make them sympathetic. Kit could not imagine telling Mom that Dusty had surfaced.

Dad had met the stunningly pretty Dusty at the country club, and astonished everybody by marrying her about a minute later. Poor Dusty was not much of a wife, companion, stepmother, or asset. She didn't even play a good game of golf, because it was an intelligent sport. Malcolm said the best sport for Dusty was probably watching them on television. Mom said often to Dad, "She has a room temperature IQ, Gavin. How on earth did you not notice before you actually married the creature?"

And it would be Kit having to say, "Dusty tries, Mom," while her three parents rolled their eyes at her.

So in the awful second divorce (because all divorces were awful; only grown-ups could pretend that divorce was easy) poor Dusty fought and pleaded and could not understand. Dusty would telephone Kit in the evening and tell Kit what was wrong in her life, and Kit would murmur comforting sounds, which was completely the wrong thing to do. Getting involved in the divorce of a parent just lengthened the nightmare.

Dad and Mom, together and separately, had instructed Kit not to speak on the phone with Dusty again. It had been months since Kit had seen Dusty.

"Oh, thank you!" cried Dusty. "Kit, carry this for me." She thrust the big white cloth-draped thing into Kit's arms. "I'm exhausted, Kit. I can hardly think, you take it, don't drop it, oh, thank you, I'll get my own cold drink, you just take care of that."

Kit Innes looked down to see what she was taking care of.

Pink and wrinkled and slumbering at the bottom of a car carrier was a brand-new baby.

Dusty clattered over the gleaming black and white tile diamonds of the entry foyer. Her footsteps were muffled in the next room, which had a heavy carpet, and then audible again on the slick wood floor of the kitchen. The water cooler bubbled as she got herself a drink.

Kit stared down at a tiny round face.

A baby!

She set the carrier on the floor and knelt to pick up the baby. Very carefully she worked one hand behind its little head, cupping its little bottom with the other, and then she lifted it. It was wearing a little terry jumpsuit, pale yellow, with a tiny Winnie-the-Pooh. She stood up slowly, holding the baby vertically, putting its little face against her throat and nestling her cheek on its sweet bald head.

The baby smelled of powder and soap. One tiny hand curled outside the blanket, and she tucked her finger inside the little fingers, and the perfection of those tiny fingers, with their lovely tiny nails, brought her almost to tears.

She was amazed by this stab of emotion for an infant she did not know.

Through the open door came a solid shaft of yellow sun, and Kit and the baby stood in it, warm and joyful. Holding her breath, she tilted the baby into the crook of her elbow so she could admire it. Its tiny face was squashed, as if there were more cheek than there was room for. The little eyes were shut, the little mouth squished outward.

The blanket that swaddled the baby was flannel, white with yellow stars. It fell to the floor when she shifted the baby, puddling softly around her ankles. Kit brushed her lips over the baby's forehead.

"This will work," said Dusty, coming up behind them. "I am so relieved! You take care of the baby, Kit, I'll be right back." She walked out of the house.

Kit rocked, crooning little compliments. "Ooooh, sweet little baby," she whispered. "You're so beautiful. What's your name, little darling? How old are you? Are you —"

The car backed out of the driveway.

Dusty was driving.

Dusty was driving away.

Kit was holding the baby.

Kit was too startled to have intelligent thoughts.

The door was still open, so Kit stepped outside and said in a normal voice, as if Dusty were still next to her, "I thought you were getting Pampers out of the car or something, Dusty. What are you doing?"

Dusty was backing into the cul-de-sac without glancing to see what might already be there.

My ex-stepmother just handed me a baby, and she's driving away.

This was so absurd that Kit looked down to double-check. Yes. It was a baby. Yes. Dusty was leaving. Kit yelled, "Dusty! Come back here!"

Dusty pressed a window button, but of course the wrong one. The back right passenger window lowered, so whatever Dusty shouted back could not be heard.

Dusty put the car in drive while she was still in reverse, so the small black sedan lurched, whipping Dusty's head back, and then she accelerated with ridiculous speed, as if entering a racetrack, and immediately had to slow down because the cul-de-sac was so short.

Then she was out of sight, and Kit Innes was standing in the sun with a very small person in her arms.

Chapter 2

Muffin Mason could not wait to be older.

But then when she got older, it didn't make any difference. No matter how much time passed, she remained shorter, skinnier, had more rules, and could not reach or see as high as her brother. All summer, Muffin had ached for school to start up again, because she would be in fourth grade. But by the end of September, she realized that was all she was in — fourth grade. Her brother, in high school, had all the fun.

And even in fourth grade, Muffin was not impressive. When they did percentiles for height and weight, Muffin was in the bottom ten percent. Compared to her sturdy classmates, she was a pencil. When they did tests for reading group, Muffin was not in the highest. When they showed off their soccer skills, Muffin had none.

This afternoon, Muffin was in the back of the family van.

Her big brother, Rowen, was in the middle.

Her parents were in the front.

Everybody was in a terrible mood.

They had just come from a high school event in which it was clear that all the kids in this entire school system were skanks and wrecks and broken glass. Mom and Dad could not imagine why they lived here. They were appalled by the disgusting students with whom Rowen seemed to be friends. They were ready to move to some other part of the country where nice people still lived.

All afternoon, Rowen kept pointing out nice kids, hoping to calm Mom and Dad down, but today the nice kids dressed in disguise and blended in perfectly with the creepy ones. Mom and Dad did not know what this world was coming to.

On the way home, Dad was out of cash and they stopped at an ATM machine — and it didn't work. It kept his card five minutes and then spit it back. "Not only do I live in a town where my son goes to school with druggies and foul-mouthed kids wearing torn obscene T-shirts," muttered Dad, "but I can't find a working ATM."

Rowen said, "Dad. All the kids you saw this afternoon are perfectly nice. You just don't like their clothes."

Rowen himself dressed beautifully. He loved looking like a catalog ad, and would practice draping a sweater the way the model wore it on page forty, and letting a suspender fall like page seventeen, slouching his socks just as they did on page eleven. "It won't help, Row," his sister, Muffin, often told him, "because you have a face like raisins in a pudding."

Actually, Rowen was quite handsome, but Muffin was always irritated with him for being so much older, so she never gave him compliments.

"You take Muffin with you when you go to Shea's tonight," said Dad. "I thought we could leave her home alone without a sitter, now that she's nine, but we can't. Not now that I've seen what kind of people this town breeds."

"Dad!" yelled Rowen. "No fair! Shea invited Kit over for me. We're going to rent movies. I don't want Muffin there."

Muffin kept quiet. She might be crummy in spelling and arithmetic, but she was smart. The way to get your way was to say nothing.

"I don't wanna baby-sit!" moaned Rowen. "Dad! Come on! Keep Muffin."

Muffin adored her cousin Shea, she adored her aunt Karen and uncle Anthony, and she adored their dogs, cats, parrot, gerbil, ferret, and water garden with fish.

She understood that she was not to get in the way, or Rowen might behave in a very uncatalog manner and smack her one, but at Shea's, staying out of the way would not be a problem, because at Shea's house everything was in the way; always. There was no order or plan; there was nothing neat or clean. There was dog and cat hair everywhere, and animals napping or exploring or running in their cages or in need of water.

This was a complete contrast to Muffin and Rowen's parents, who were very neat. It was impossible to believe that her mom and Aunt Karen were sisters. Mom especially did not believe it.

Mom and Dad had spent a ton of money on their house, and their wallpaper, and their chairs and table, and their house was going to stay clean and sparkling and beautiful — and it did. If you played a game on

Mom's dining room table, you cleaned it up and counted the pieces.

Whereas at Shea's house, you couldn't find the game. If you did locate it, it was missing the board.

Vaguely Muffin heard her brother continue his argument that a nine-year-old would absolutely ruin an evening of three sixteen-year-olds.

But in the Mason household, Dad always won. It was remarkable. One year, Row kept score. But there was no score. Dad was the only player. It was like living with the weather. If Dad rained, you got wet.

So when Dad said Muffin would go with Row to Shea's house for the evening, she was going with Rowen to Shea's.

Kit Innes heard herself laughing in a peculiar detached way, like a recording behind a television show.

The sun was glaring on the translucent skin of the tiny baby. The baby was not actually bald, but had a fine down of almost invisible hair. When Kit brushed her cheek against the baby's, it was like brushing velvet.

She went into the house, closing the front door with her foot.

The stuffy dark of the house had disappeared. Dusty racing through and the burble of the water cooler and the warmth of the baby had taken care of that.

Kit looked down. Perhaps this was a very lifelike doll. Dusty did collect dolls. Dusty loved the full-page magazine ads where you pulled the card from the magazine and ordered a beautiful shelf doll for $59.95 a month for four months. When Dusty had lived here, one entire bedroom had been filled with dolls. Dusty never played with them, though, and her reasons for collecting them had never been clear. Dusty liked the act of buying things, and once she'd bought something it had no use; she was bored and had to go buy another.

It was clear that this was not a doll.

With no warning, its little chest heaved. It made a croaky sound, not the soft coo Kit would have expected. More like a frog. Its little back arched, and its miniature feet pressed down on Kit's waist, not as if the baby were trying to stand, but as if a convulsion were coming on.

Kit was terrified. What was she supposed to do?

What if it died? What was that horrible thing babies got, that sudden infant death thing? How did you know? Should she call an ambulance? Why was its little chest jerking around, both getting air and not getting air?

"Come on, baby, take a good breath. You can do it," she crooned, hoping that babies did not sense fear the way attack dogs did.

The baby breathed deeply. Its little head sagged so fast that Kit had to catch it in her palm, so it wouldn't snap off. It seemed to lose its spine, and turned into a Beanie Baby, all sag and no bone.

Kit felt the same.

Cradling the baby very carefully, so it would not notice that anything was happening and react by suffocating itself, Kit walked into the family room. Here the decorator had gone huge: huge furniture, huge shelves, huge jugs and baskets, and a huge collection of duck decoys, although Dad had certainly never hunted a duck. Dad hunted movie concepts.

The wall of windows was high above the seventeenth hole, with a view of water hazards, artfully planted trees, and a sweet little curve of bridge. If a golfer was going to behave badly and swear at his game, it was here.

To Kit's right was a stretch of long thin glass cabinets — the romantic British butler look that some people might refer to as a kitchen. Dad did not cook. He hardly ever had food around. If Kit stayed over here more than a day or two, Mom packed a picnic basket. Sometimes she would send a thermos of Dad's favorite coffee, which was when Kit wanted to know why they hadn't just stayed married, and Mom wanted to know why Kit had to bring *that* up again, and it took all Kit's self-control not to develop an attitude.

Anyway, Dad was an eating-out kind of guy, so the room was not really a kitchen, but just an extension of the family room that happened to have appliances and sinks.

The baby stirred. Its little face stretched out of shape and its body quivered, as if on the verge of a sneeze, and then it sank back with a burble and slept with its tiny mouth open.

Kit was already exhausted and she had not been in charge of this baby for two minutes.

She didn't think the baby was literally a newborn. It didn't have the wrinkled, red, rashy look of being brand-new. It looked softer and a little rounded, as if it had had a week or two to get used to the world. But Kit doubted the baby was as old as one month.

She balanced the tiny body in the crook

of her left arm, and with her right hand she spread the flannel blanket across the middle portion of the sofa. The decorator had chosen a leather couch, dyed hunter green to give it a British library look, crusted with brass studs. Kit lowered the baby into the dip of the sofa, where the seat met the back, so the baby could not roll over and fall off. Although it looked like an awfully young baby for knowing how to roll.

The moment it left the warmth of her arm, the baby woke up.

Its eyes opened so wide that Kit giggled, and the baby stared not at her, the source of the giggle, but straight up, as if its eyes didn't go left and right yet. It gurgled, a much sweeter sound than the frog croaks. Its feet began to wave, as if the baby thought feet were hands.

Kit's father was very big on photographs. Perhaps it was his Hollywood attitude, or perhaps all fathers are big on photographs of their children. By Kit's estimate, Dad had taken a million snapshots of her, and a thousand movies. Dad believed every event, no matter how minor, must be immortalized. He still photographed her at the airport, arriving and departing, each and every visit she made to him in California. Fearful that he would miss a minute of her life, he handed a pack of cameras to Mom and Malcolm whenever he left New Jersey for a longer stretch than usual.

Dad had a collection of very impressive, very expensive cameras, but everybody else was afraid of them. There was too much adjusting to do, and too much fear of breakage or loss. So for years now, he'd been buying disposable cameras by the dozen and ordering people to use them in his absence. So, sitting on the counter in the unused kitchen was a stack of cameras, all still in their bright yellow cardboard boxes.

Now the baby was waving all four limbs, giving it more in common with upside-down turtles than with humans. Kit opened a camera, peeled away the foil, and took a flash photo. And because she had been brought up to believe in quantity, she took five more. Whatever angle she used, the baby was adorable.

She had been afraid of the baby to start with, because it was so little and so unexpected. But now she saw that the baby was beautiful. Even though the baby seemed fine lying in the slant of the sofa, Kit had to pick it up again. She nuzzled its face and tummy. "Go back to sleep, little sweetie," she crooned. “Mommy will be back in a minute, Mommy will be —”

And then she thought:

How do I know Dusty will be back in a minute?

For that matter, how do I know Dusty is the mommy?

Chapter 3

Dusty drove away with good intentions. She had a mental list of things that must be accomplished swiftly and in the proper order.

But handing the baby to Kit was such a relief.

Babies were enormously difficult. You could think of nothing else.

And Dusty was accustomed to thinking of her own body, not some little twenty-inch, eight-pound body. (She'd had a cat that size once, but the cat took care of himself. The baby, now — it most definitely would not take care of itself. It had not once slept more than two hours at a time, and sometimes it slept only ten minutes!)

She had gotten quite cross with the baby for refusing to sleep during the night. And not only did it stay awake, it would not lie peacefully in the little bassinet at the motel room. It whined and whimpered and croaked. Some nights not even picking the baby up and rocking and cuddling it would soothe it. Sometimes it just kept on crying.

It was so annoying to be backed into a corner. Dusty liked a world where all the choices were hers. She was determined to make this work out her way, no matter who got stubborn and difficult.

The rental car drove smoothly, and she found a nice calm radio station and listened to nice calm music. That was boring, so she found hard rock, and began dancing her arms and shoulders to the music. She had ten pounds to lose! The weight horrified Dusty. Having a baby was not good for your figure. Or your stamina. Or your complexion. Or anything that Dusty could tell.

She drove past the turn she'd meant to take.

She noticed it half a mile later.

Dusty had found that if she looked hard enough, she could always see that things were meant. Now she realized that Kit, who never went to her father's house when Gavin was in California, had been *brought* to the house just to help her, Dusty. It was meant for Kit to be standing in the door just when Dusty expected the house to be empty. So it was *meant* for Kit to take care of the baby.

And who could be better at such a task?

Kit had her father's strong will and decisive manner (and none of her mother's unfriendly attitude). Kit was terribly reliable.

Dusty kept driving.

The sky was so blue and the sun so yellow and the day so warm.

She thought, I deserve some time to myself. I didn't ask things to work out like this, and it's way too hard. I've been struggling with this baby and this situation for seventeen days now. I will get my hair done and have a facial, and I'll charge an outfit that fits, so I don't feel fat. Something with style, maybe in that new shade of plum, and then I'll go to the aromatherapist. I need to lavish attention on myself for a change. It just isn't good for you to give up all your space and energy. You must take time for yourself.

Dusty felt better. She loved thinking of her Self, which felt like a person zipped inside her, whom she could admire and be glad about. But not when her hair was nasty and her stomach sagged and she had been up all night with a baby who would not improve.

Once her hair was done, she would face her problems. You could do anything if your hair looked good. Kit was lucky, her hair always looked good.

Dusty loved when things worked out so well.

Kit stroked the baby's wrist, which made its hand curl. She set her index finger in its palm, and three miniature fingers covered her own long polished fingernail.

Dusty had been frazzled and exhausted, not surprising if she had just had a baby. Even if she had had this baby a couple or three weeks ago. But whether or not you were a mess, did you hand your new baby over to your ex-stepdaughter and drive away?

Why would you sob and gasp and yank at doors trying to get your sleeping baby out of a car?

Why would you take this baby to a house you did not live in? A house that technically was closed to you?

Had Dusty expected Dad to be here? She hadn't acted that way. If Dusty had found the house empty and used the key that apparently Dad had not gotten around to collecting from her, what had she planned on doing? Was she going to live here for a while? Suppose Kit hadn't been here. Could Dusty — even Dusty! — have planned to leave the baby alone in the house, while she drove off on this errand she had to do?

The thought of a tiny baby alone in a large stale hotel of a house made Kit's skin crawl.

The image of Dusty driving away, leaving a baby in an empty house, made Kit gag.

Dusty had not even told Kit the baby's name. Or whether it was a boy or a girl.

It didn't seem like the thing a mother would do with her new baby.

So . . . was Dusty the mother?

Or . . . was Dusty the baby-sitter? In which case the real mommy had not made a wise decision in caretakers.

Or . . . neither one? In which case . . . whose baby was this?

First Muffin and Row stopped at the video store so her brother could rent the movies that he and Shea and Kit were going to watch.

Muffin had complete faith that these would be the kind of movies she was not allowed to watch. There would be hours of violence and screaming and people leaping from buildings and saving one another from maniacs and firing their machine guns and rescuing the world. Muffin would be tucked up in her kangaroo sleeping bag on the floor and would feel safe and wonderful in the half dark, with the teenagers talking, and Shea dancing to herself, because Shea danced to herself the way other people sang to themselves or talked to themselves, and the dogs sharing the tacos, and the cats sleeping on her feet to keep her safe.

Muffin did not know Kit, but Row had pointed her out at school events. He found her very appealing. To Muffin, Kit had seemed a speck boring, as if Kit were the type who really did spend her time carefully listening, rather than busily thinking her own interesting thoughts. Row said that meant Kit was a nicer person than Muffin, since Muffin never listened. Although, he added, that was not difficult; everybody was nicer and more desirable than his sister.

Row picked up bags of chips at the counter (Fritos, Doritos, honey mustard pretzels, and sour cream potato chips), although you never had to worry about food at Aunt Karen and Uncle Anthony's.

Shea's family had much better food than Muffin's family.

Muffin's mom was very healthy. Health was a favorite topic for her. She drank only herbal teas, and took special medications made from the centers of important flowers, and had a daily dose of seaweed to purify herself. She bought bread at a particular grocery, and vegetables from another, and she cooked with great care, so that they never needed salt or butter, but just the flavor of the vegetable.

Muffin's dad didn't pay any attention to this when he was at work. He mainly had cheeseburgers and french fries and vanilla shakes for lunch. Every night he fibbed to Mom and said he had had no salt and no cholesterol, and every night Mom seemed to believe this. Even when she was the one to clean the old McDonald's bags out of the car, she believed they had just flown in and had nothing to do with Dad.

In matters of nutrition, Muffin did not disobey her mom. She actually ate her little baby carrots in their plastic lunch bag; and she actually had her yogurt and her organic plums and her seven-grain bread with homemade peanut butter.

But at Shea's, it would be impossible to pay attention to Mom's food theories, because Shea's family were the junk-food champions. There was nothing they didn't have, and it would all be open, so you didn't have to be the one actually ripping the package apart. There would be a dozen packages on the counter, clipped at the top with colored bag clips to keep things crisp and greasy and salty and yummy, and in the freezer many kinds of ice cream would already have one scoop out of them, and in the refrigerator leftovers would beckon, and in the bread box, there was never bread. There were cupcakes and chocolate-covered doughnuts.

Muffin thought happily of shedding pets and yummy chips and violent movies and staying up late.

Kit should be doing something sensible, but one of Dusty's characteristics was the ability to make everybody around her equally dumb.

The house hummed.

Appliances and air-conditioning talked gently.

Kit felt as if she were visiting distant relatives. She could think of nothing to do but sit on the sofa and watch the baby sleep.

Dusty did not come back.

Kit went to the front hall to check the carrier. Yes, inside the carrier, under a second baby blanket, was a packet of newborn diapers, some baby wipes, a pack of disposable bottles, and a six-pack of ready-mix formula. She toted the whole thing into the family room and set it on the floor next to the baby. The huge green sofa made a wall between the baby and the big picture windows that faced the golf course.

There was something new in the room along with the baby.

There was a distinctly unpleasant smell.

Terrific, thought Kit. Baby-sitting should be restricted to clean events. Oh, well. At least I have a pack of newborn-size Huggies.

The little terrycloth jumper the baby had on unsnapped between the legs and out the back. She peeled it away, and released its tiny curled feet into the air. The paper diaper was so small she burst out laughing. It was fastened with little tapes. When she tugged at them, the diaper fell open.

It was a boy.

"Hello, little guy," she whispered to him. "What's your name, little sweetheart? Tell me your name."

She mopped him up with a baby wipe, which wasn't too bad after all, and then realized she'd tossed the diaper out before seeing exactly how it worked. Handily the diaper pack had illustrated instructions. Four steps.

"Stretch sides and elastic in back," she muttered, and sure enough, this mini paper garment had stretch sides and elastic, which she stuck under the baby's bottom, and then little grippers to hold the back to the front.

He liked having his feet free, and waved them eagerly. If Kit had been lying on her back and waving her feet around like that, it would have been aerobic exercise to die from, but the baby was just enjoying himself.

"You need a name, kid," she said to him. She tucked his tiny feet back in the little footed jumpsuit and snapped the legs up. Then she stroked his cheek and instantly he turned to her finger and tried to get it into his mouth.

"Do you want something to eat, little guy?" she said. "Are you trying to give me instructions?"

She studied the available materials. A long slim plastic envelope got stuck down into a plastic bottle, and the envelope edges lapped over the bottle top. Then you opened the fliptop of a can of Similac With Iron Infant Formula, which sounded right (and smelled disgusting), and poured some into the bottle. Then you fit a nipple into a screw top and fastened the whole thing down. The formula was room temperature, so Kit decided she didn't have to heat it.

If I were this kid's mother, thought Kit, the last thing I would do is leave him with me. I don't know how or when to do anything.

"What's your name, fella?" she said to him.

He was squalling. This was definitely an instruction. Get that bottle in my mouth! he was yelling.

She rested his little head on the crook of her left arm, his feet dangling off the end of her left hand. The nipple seemed large enough for a colt, and she was scared it would choke him. But after a minute of scrabbling and failure, the baby remembered how this was done. He chugged down his milk with concentration, a little man with a major task.

"You're a serious guy. You need a solid name," she told him. "I'm going to call you Sam. Sam the Baby."

Kit's mother was crazy about babies. Mom ran the nursery on Sunday morning while the parents were in church. She'd cuddle and sing and rock the babies and tots, and of course get to miss the sermon, which she despised anyway. (Mom did not like advice, one reason she hadn't stayed married to Dad: Dad gave advice solidly. Kit rarely paid attention; Mom paid too much and got mad; and poor Dusty paid lots of attention, but missed the point and did the wrong things.)

Mom burped her nursery babies, an event that in grown-ups would be embarrassing, but in babies was adorable, so Kit carefully propped the baby on her shoulder and patted his tiny back. Sure enough, a hiccupy thwop of a burp filled the room with gassy, milky scent and the baby turned soft and pliable against her, and Kit was in love.

She held him again in the crook of her arm, and he had one more swallow, and then fell asleep, completely and instantly, the nipple falling from his mouth, milk draining onto his chin.

She wrapped him in his flannel blanket and put him carefully back in the slant of the sofa. Then she lowered herself next to him. "So, Sam the Baby," she said softly, and in spite of herself she came very close to a sob, "so — who is your daddy, Sam?"

* * *

It was a very old Cadillac, once black and now a sort of aged bronze. The driver hated his car. He hated it so intensely that whenever he drove, he wanted to smash it. He could easily have driven through the plate glass of stores and when he drove, he like to pick out cars that he would crash into on purpose — except that he had to keep this car in working condition.

Every time he had to pour gas into its greedy gullet, he hated the car.

Every time he had to change the oil, he hated the car.

And today, driving up and around every one of the endless stupid identical dead ends of this stupid golf course development, he knew that his car was not as nice as the cars of people who picked up the trash on this street, never mind the people who lived here. If anybody was home (although this was not the kind of place where people stayed home; they bought mansions and then they went out to work or to play golf) they would see his ugly smeared old car, one step from the junkyard, and they would narrow their eyes. What's he doing in our road? they would think. We don't have losers here.

And now Dusty had ruined everything.

Money had been there. Enough money

for both of them. He would have had the best car; the car of his dreams! But she was greedy. She wouldn't settle for the original amount, and she certainly wouldn't settle for less. He wanted the money so bad. And without Dusty, he could get nothing.

He was done with having nothing. He would get Dusty. He would get that money.

She had to hole up someplace and her ex-husband had a house in this Seven Hills place, empty almost all the time. If he could just remember where it was!

Even though they were architect-designed houses, supposedly full of personality and excitement, they looked exactly alike. Each had a little knobby row of green bushes around the foundation, and a single spindly maple to the left of the brick sidewalk and three white birches clumped on the right. Their grass got more attention than he had gotten in his entire life.

Okay, Dusty, he thought. Where are you?

But he was not really having thoughts. He was having rage.

Dad and Dusty had split a year ago.

Kit's goal had been to keep herself bland and even.

When Mom left Dad for Malcolm, Kit had been so fiercely angry that she was afraid of herself. She was afraid of how much noise she would make if she started screaming. Afraid of the terrible words she would use to Mom. Afraid of throwing things, and breaking them; of throwing them directly at her very own beloved mother.

And so Kit gave herself Dullness Training. She succeeded. The key was in facial expression. No excessive movement of mouth or lips; no wrinkling of the forehead; no flinging the body around; and above all, no emotions that would make the eyes prickle with tears or the fingers clench.

Vocabulary had to be reduced. Kit preferred the basics: *how are you*, *thank you*, and *please* were fine. This prevented Kit from screaming names at the mother who had ended their happy lives, the stepfather she didn't like because he'd been willing to have an affair with a married woman, and the father she adored — but was even more mad at, because he would not fight back. If that's what your mother wants, that's what she may have, Dad would say.

Although she had kept her grades up, because Kit liked studying, in all other ways she concentrated on being average.

Sometimes when she was thinking of getting a tattoo of spiderwebs on her cheek, just to show these three grown-ups what she thought of their behavior, she would catch a glimpse of herself in a mirror — an okay, bland, acceptable girl who looked as if her biggest conflict was deciding whether to have cornflakes or Cheerios.

Kit was in the midst of being dull when Shea took up with her. Shea (and Shea's exhausting family, pets, and hobbies) was exciting, wild, difficult, creative, and noisy. And now Shea's cousin Row wanted to hang out with them. Shea said Row had a crush on Kit. Kit could not imagine this, because she felt far too blank and blah for anybody to like her that much. On whom did he have this crush? Her former, and possibly future, self — as active and exciting as Shea? Or her present self, the only one he had ever seen — as predictable and dull a girl as ever inhabited a high school?

Kit had come to Dad's house for a favorite California sweatshirt. It featured a scary rock-band silhouette in glittering copper and raised evil black. With black tights and the sweatshirt, she could dance through the movies the way Shea danced, and maybe this was what Rowen Mason wanted.

And maybe not.

Kit did not really want to let go of her bland, boring self. It was a satisfying little person, easily managed, and she liked her small vocabulary, and her short range of expression. She did not want to count back nine months, or maybe ten, depending on how old Sam the Baby was, to figure out what her father and Dusty might have been doing.

She had charge of this kid now, this infant, this sweet sleeping creature, and she did not want him to be her half-brother. She did not want to have to get furious and shrieking over this — that her father had gone and had another kid, and not bothered with it? Or not even known about it? Or forgotten?

What was it with grown-ups?

They were so horribly, horrifically, constantly selfish.

This morning, Kit had felt even, as if she were balanced; and she had tonight with Shea and Row to think about; and she refused to have a raging fury at her various families take over her calm body.

So I will consider this calmly, she told herself, as if this were average and happened in all families.

Nine months back was January.

The new year had opened with new snow, and fresh plans, and high hopes. All came to nothing. Sophomore year had been so hard for Kit. It was just endurance, like entering the Iditarod without meaning to. When she arrived at the end of last year, that awful school year, still alive and able to talk, Kit had been amazed.

She was so relieved to be a junior this fall. Junior year was so civilized. Junior year she was a young woman with a future. She had not entirely figured out how to approach her future in a calm and reasoned manner, so she had decided against being in the drama production, but she did agree to be in charge of ushers. She played flute in the concert band, deep in the second row, and had agreed to be in the marching band, since there were so many flutes she was invisible in the crowd. She loved marching band: The uniform was flashy, even spectacular, like the personality Kit felt she would have if she ever decided to have a personality again. She joined the Winter Club, which took weekend trips (downhill, cross-country, skating, snowmobiling, and even ice fishing), because there was no parent there to observe her, and with several hundred miles between her and the parents, she thought she might let go of her calm. Privately, that is. Nothing to be exhibited at home.

Shea had become a best friend. Kit had pretty much accepted that dull people only had acquaintances, and so she was thrilled to have a close friendship again. As for dating Shea's cousin Row, she was afraid of the whole thing. Shea insisted that just being in the same room, just sharing a bowl of popcorn, would allow Kit to slide easily and pleasantly into being a couple with Row.

Row had decided that Shea and Kit could not last another week without seeing three particular movies, films absolutely necessary to being real teenagers in a real decade. They'd have to stay up all night watching them.

Rowen's mother said not at their house, and Kit's mother said not at her house, but Shea's mother said you can always party here. Everything was always okay with Shea's mother as long as it happened while she was standing there. However, Shea's mother was the kind of person you didn't do anything in front of except eat popcorn.

Kit felt herself moving in the direction of tears, which were against all her rules. She wanted tonight to go just right. She wanted to be the Kit that Rowen Mason had a crush on. And what if Dusty didn't get back in time? Well, that was ridiculous, Kit wasn't going to Shea's until dinnertime. Hours.

This isn't crucial, she told herself. Figuring out Sam the Baby is. So. Think.

Last winter, Dad had been consumed by a three-night miniseries he was putting together when miniseries had gone out of fashion, so it was risky. It had been filmed in Canada. Except for forty-eight hours at Christmas, Dad had not been on the East Coast from mid-December till mid-February. And on Christmas Eve, Kit had yelled at him for being more involved with his work than with her, and he yelled back that she had a perfectly good stepfather for emergencies such as these.

She remembered hating Dad for implying that Malcolm could substitute for her own father; hating Dad for joking about it; hating all parents and grown-ups everywhere for taking divorce so lightly. She remembered that she had laughed in a friendly way and let it go, because that was how dull bland people handled distress.

"Anyway," Dad had said, and Kit thought it had been during that same conversation, "being with Dusty gives me hives."

So it seemed unlikely that Dad was the daddy of Sam the Baby.

On the other hand, Dusty had not *always* given Dad allergies.

The old Caddy tried yet another road along the golf course.

The driver's fury crawled into his hands and into his grip on the wheel, and sank through his body to the soles of his right foot, the one resting on the gas pedal, and he yearned to drive across the yards, and crush the perfect little flowers, maybe take out a pet if he could move fast enough.

He had been at the house of Dusty's ex-husband just once. The front hall was open to the second floor, with stairs for a bride to come down, as Dusty had, and over the stairs was a peculiar cut-lemon-shaped window that Dusty thought incredibly beautiful and rare. If he could find the house with the lemon window over the front door . . .

A cat ran across the street in front of him.

He veered, trying to hit it, but missed.

It was a good thing he'd tried, though. From this angle, with the sun glinting against it, he spotted the flared lemon slices of glass.

He drove back down the short little dead-end road, smiling to himself.

There was no car in the driveway. That meant she had put her car in the garage and closed it, so it would look as if she had not come here. But he was too smart for Dusty; he had always been too smart for Dusty.

He could not let Dusty get away. Dusty always assumed that money problems would work out, and for her they always did. But for him they never did, and this was his chance at money, and she was in the way. She had to obey him. He was going to have that money, and he did not care what Dusty wanted.

He parked at an angle, filling the driveway so that she could not drive her car out of the garage no matter which door she opened.

When the phone rang, Kit knew it was her mother, checking to see why picking up a sweatshirt had lasted so long. Mom would have been expecting her to come in the screen-porch door ages ago.

I have to answer the phone, thought Kit. Otherwise Mom will fly into a panic. But if I answer it, what do I say?

Hi, I'm baby-sitting for a kid whose

name I've made up, but don't worry, he had his bottle, and Dusty is probably his mother, although she drove away, which is not a good sign, but don't worry, she's bound to come back eventually. Don't worry, he's probably not my half-brother, because I did talk to Dad twice this week, and if he had just become a father, wouldn't he have mentioned it?

Kit felt jumpy, as if her very own mother were a threat to the baby.

"Hi, honey. I thought you were coming home right away," said her mother. "Couldn't you find the sweatshirt?"

She had the odd reaction of loving her mother very intensely, a feeling which did not come that often anymore. Her mother's voice sounded very mellow and sweet; a woman who was a perfect mother, who cared wonderfully for babies, but who had gotten a little slack with a teenager.

"I'm just poking around," said Kit in her cultivated dull voice. "I ended up reading a book I left here last time. I'll be home in a while." She felt a queer little pinch of pleasure that she still sounded so dull and boring when she was in the midst of a real mystery that might hugely disrupt their lives.

Sam the Baby, without appearing to

wake up, snuffled a little and then croaked froggily. Then he sagged so far into his sleep it looked deeper than any sleep Kit had ever had. He was beautiful. His body and his sleep were both beautiful.

Kit walked to the far end of the kitchen, her hand muffling the receiver. She was in danger of wanting to keep Sam the Baby. She might do something stupid like beg Dad to remarry Dusty, or try to convince Mom and Malcolm to let Dusty and the baby live in the guest room.

"Okay," said her mother. "Do you want to go to Lord & Taylor's with me or not?"

There was a sale on their favorite brand of shoes. They had planned to go shoe shopping. There was nothing Mom liked more than trying on lots of shoes and not buying them.

"I guess not. Let me know what they have around."

"Okay," said Mom cheerfully. "See you later. Or are you going straight over to Shea's?"

"Probably straight over to Shea's. We're watching movies all night and then tomorrow's Sunday and we'll sleep all morning."

"See you tomorrow, then," said Mom, "probably by noon, okay? Bye, darling." Mom moved quickly. She would scoop up her purse and car keys and be out the door in twenty seconds. Nor could Kit change her mind about telling Mom, because Mom refused to have a car phone; she listened to mystery novels on tape and didn't like the action interrupted.

Kit Innes, who had so carefully given in to all decisions of all grown-ups, had just made a large decision. She had kept the presence of Sam the Baby a secret.

Was she half protecting somebody? Dusty? Dad?

"You are not Dad's son," she told Sam the Baby. "You are not my half-brother. I am not going to call up Dad in California and say, 'So, Dad? How should I handle this interesting situation?' "

Anyway, it wouldn't be a situation for long. Dusty would drive around, get lost, get found, forget what she'd been planning to do, and come for the baby.

The doorbell rang.

It was the kind of bell that kept going as long as you leaned on it, and Dusty leaned on it. Kit left the sleeping baby safely in his slant and went to the front door to let Dusty in.

Chapter 4

Kit was thinking that this time she would let go, and she would tell Dusty exactly what she thought. This gave Kit a hundred things to yell at Dusty. Maybe a thousand.

"What kind of mother are you?" she would start. "You tell me one thing so important you had to drive away without even telling me how to take care of him! Or when to feed him! Or even what his name is! And I demand to know who the father is. Is it my father? Don't you fib to me, Dusty. I'll see right through you. I know you. You can't —"

Why was Dusty ringing the doorbell?

Dusty had a key.

She never rang doorbells, anyway, because she could never find the button, and she believed any electronic communication was unfriendly. You should just pound on the door, calling, "Hi, it's me, it's Dusty, I'm here!"

So even as Kit was releasing the door, she knew she was a fool.

But the door was already open and a foot was already in it. A large dark brown shoe was halfway into the hall, the kind of shoe that was meant to be shiny leather, but this shoe had not been polished in a long time and was scuffed almost through to the sock.

Kit squared her foot on her side of the door, preventing it from opening farther. She was nose to nose with some man who had expected just to walk in. Some man who was stunned to see her. He had expected someone else to open this door.

She knew him from somewhere. But she could make no connection. For all she knew, she recognized him from *America's Most Wanted.*

He was grotesquely sweaty and in need of a shave. The collar of his shirt was so worn that frayed cotton laced his neck. His hair was bristled and sharp, as if he'd had his hair cut only a minute before. He'd had a bad complexion as a boy, and deep pockmarks were spattered across his face.

There were some good things about Dullness Training. Kit's expression did not change and her face did not show fear. As a matter of fact, she didn't feel fear; she just knew that she ought to.

"Dusty here?" he said. He was breathing hard, as if he'd been running but his car was in the drive. An old scary car; a car so long and low it seemed to have driven through other times.

He tried to see past her into the house. She had a sick sense that he knew where to look; that he had been here before. Perhaps this awful man and Dusty had been here when Dad was not. Perhaps this house really *was* a hotel and there really *were* strangers staying in the same rooms, sleeping in the same beds, using the same towels.

Not fear but nausea crawled over Kit.

"Dusty!" he yelled into the house when Kit didn't answer him.

She could taste the beer he'd had when he breathed in her face. "Dusty?" she said, as blandly as possible. It worked with him the way it worked with all grown-ups. He became uncertain. But he did not take his hand off the doorknob. His body was scrawny, but the hand was fat and puffy, the heavy yellow fingernails ridged and torn back into the quick.

They were both leaning against the door,

he trying to open, she trying to close.

"You mean my ex-stepmother?" Kit shifted to prevent him from seeing anything. But there was nothing to see. The decorator had not been able to think of much to do in the big front hall, except glossy black and white tiles set at angles, and one long skinny table with no purpose.

"She should be here." The man couldn't stand still, but was peering to the left of her, peering to the right of her. His eyes darted separately, as if he were coming apart. Kit thought he must be on something; some drug was separating his seams.

Dusty, too, had been coming apart.

How did Sam the Baby fit into this? Two frayed, frantic, coming-apart grown-ups — and a newborn?

Now she felt the first edge of fear. Fear for Sam.

"Dusty's my cousin," the man said next, and now Kit remembered him; he had appeared at the wedding, a deeply upsetting event nobody could believe was happening. After three or four months, Dad couldn't believe it had happened, either. Kit had perfected her dullness by then, and so had stood calmly with her flowers, calmly observing that every single grown-up except

Dad thought this was insane. She could not remember what the cousin's role had been.

She didn't want to ask his name; they might have to shake hands. She did not want to touch him.

"Listen, it doesn't matter about Dusty," he said. "I've just come for the baby."

He had come for Sam the Baby?

This pockmarked, fat-fingered man with torn shoes, infected fingernails, beer breath, and driving a ruined carcass of an automobile? She was supposed to turn Sam the Baby, tiny helpless Sam, over to this? Sam, whom she had cuddled and changed and fed, and who might be her very own brother? To this scum?

Kit felt such fury at Dusty that it collected in her eyes. She was blind with it. She had not felt this way since Mom had moved out to live with Malcolm years ago. She had been a child. Now she collected her calm and her dull as if they were asteroids flying about in space. "What baby?" she said to the cousin, her mouth drooping open to show confusion.

He dropped the doorknob, stepping back and squinting at her. She did not slam the door but inched it forward, occupying the space with her body, making it awkward for him to touch the door again.

"I don't think Dusty left anything here," said Kit. "I helped her pack."

Now she began closing the door. So far, Sam had not made a sound. Any minute he might start, and large as the house was, distant as Sam on the green couch was, his little croaks would be distinctive.

"Dusty didn't just drive up here?" he said. His mouth twitched, rippling over his teeth, and she could not tell if he wanted to sob or scream. Then his fist clenched and she knew he wanted to scream.

So did Kit. She had to get this door closed and locked. She said, "We haven't seen Dusty in months."

She remembered his name, suddenly. Dusty's maiden name was Bing. Dusty Bing — it never sounded like a name, really; more like a mistake on everybody's part. Her cousin was Ed. This man was Ed Bing.

"Oh," he said. "I guess I was mistaken." He backed up, much as Dusty had backed her car, without looking behind him. He didn't trip. "Sorry I bothered you."

Kit shut the door, turning the deadbolt so fast that the knob slammed her finger.

Now the house was a fortress — the only way in would be to smash a window.

She redistributed her calm, felt rational

again, and now it crossed her mind Dusty might have *sent* Ed Bing. He was her cousin, after all. How like Dusty to send the wrong person on the wrong errand and have him say the wrong things!

She peered back out the door. Ed Bing hadn't driven away yet. Should she just go ask him what was going on? But she didn't want him to know about Sam, and besides —

Kit had a sense of movement at the corner of her eyes, and whirled toward the living room windows, but nothing was there. A muffled rasp came from outdoors, like branches scraping the house. Kit slanted forward and through the dining room windows saw Ed Bing moving along the side of the house, brushing against the shrubs.

What if Ed and Dusty really did use this house as a hotel? What if this man had keys to the other doors? What if —

Kit slid into the formal dining room. Nobody dined here. It smelled of furniture polish, not flowers or food. Ed Bing circled Dad's house. He walked right up onto the slate terrace, right up to the window wall of the family room. He actually cupped his hands around his eyes to see past the glare and then he stared around the room.

The baby lay hidden by the high green leather of the sofa back.

But was the carrier hidden?

Ed Bing could see something. He kept arching his back and angling himself to get a better view. He knew she was right here! How could he trespass like this! With his footsteps and with his eyes! There was nothing calm about him. For a moment Kit thought he was going to put his fist through the plate glass and she even had time to plan her actions: Let him bleed to death; grab the baby and run out the other door.

The part of her that wasn't thinking — or maybe the part that was — slipped into the kitchen and picked up a disposable camera.

She shot him as he turned away, and again as he walked off. She ran to the front window and snapped his car. Then she flattened herself against the wall so he wouldn't see her as he emerged from the far side of the house.

He got into his car and slammed the door with enough force to unhinge it. Or unhinge his mind. He backed out of the driveway and, looking around, backed up more, until the island of flowers in the middle of the turnaround was between him and the way out. Then he slammed the gas down, driving on purpose over the flowers, yanking the car wheels from side to side so they totally crushed the little garden.

As he bounced down off the curb, a red zinnia caught in the license plate.

Muffin was very grumpy with her brother. "You had no right to do that!" she shouted at him.

"Just get in the backseat," said Rowen.

"What did you have to go and have a fight with Shea for?" demanded Muffin. "I didn't have a fight with Shea. Let me stay here. I don't care what you do. Shea's my cousin, too, I don't have to have you along."

"We're not staying," said Rowen irritably. "She's too annoying."

"What are we going to do?" said Muffin. As usual, she had not been listening. She did not know what the argument with Shea had been about or who had been right, although in the case of her cousin and her brother, Muffin had observed that usually neither one of them was right.

She must not cry. That would irritate Row a whole, whole lot, and they did have to be together all evening. She must convince Row to cool off by driving around

(Row loved driving without going anywhere). Then she would convince Row to go to Shea's after all.

Muffin took off her seat belt and her shoes and flopped down on the floor of the car. She liked how the raised pipework in the middle arched her back. She put her feet up against the windows and wiggled her socks at invisible cars. She liked staring out the windows and seeing only the tops of things and not being able to recognize anything.

She liked not being able to see her brother, who wasn't worth seeing.

The sun cast its gold on the big back windows, so the half-moon prints of Ed Bing's cupped hands were as visible as etchings. Kit wanted to find paper towels and Windex him off her windows, but Sam the Baby began to cry.

It was a skinny undernourished little weep, which conversely filled Kit entirely. There was no appetite in her now to fret about a creepy cousin and whatever stupid strategy Dusty had in mind, sending Ed Bing around.

She drew the drapes, set the baby and his stuff into the carrier, hefted the whole thing, and got it upstairs to her own bedroom. The baby's eyes flew open much wider but didn't focus. His little face crumpled in distress. His cry gained volume and became a true sob. A wrenching noise, maybe the worst Kit had ever heard, because every sob was her responsibility.

She had meant to examine the bedroom for evidence of Dusty or strangers or creepy cousins using it as their hotel, but she forgot.

"You know, Sam the Baby, if you're going to be Dusty's son, you're going to have to be tough stuff. Here you are only a minute old, or a week, or a month, and Dusty's wandering around the state somewhere. She didn't even remember to introduce you. So toughen up, kid." She read the back of the formula bottle to see if she could still use what was left in the bottle, but she couldn't. She should have refrigerated the open bottle, so she fixed a new one. After hardly an ounce (it was marked on the side of the bottle), Sam the Baby slept again, little mouth fallen open, little chin damp.

She eased the baby onto her bedspread, kissing him. Oh, Dusty! she thought. Dusty, you're so lucky! He is so beautiful!

They lay together on her bed while she

admired Sam's perfection — his beautiful little flat nose and curly mini-hands.

Should Kit telephone Shea? Let her know that things were not on schedule? But Shea was the kind of busy person who, if Kit came at six o'clock or at eight, would be fine about it because Shea's own projects wrapped up when they wrapped up, and not according to what she might have told other people. Shea did not live in the kind of household where anybody even remembered to change clocks for daylight saving until they had been late or early ten days in a row. So there was no need to alarm Shea.

Kit would baby-sit and everything would be normal in a minute or two, because Dusty would be back and have an explanation for this.

When Kit woke up, an hour had passed.

She and the baby had napped peacefully. She woke up with her heart racing.

What if Dusty had kidnapped Sam the Baby?

No.

Dusty was dim and half wired, but she wasn't bad.

This was her son, and the reason she looked so awful was that she'd recently given birth. An event known to be tiring.

Unless the reason she looked so awful was that the baby wasn't hers, and Ed Bing was her partner in crime.

Kit sprawled over the bed and grabbed her remote.

New Jersey News came on public television at six. Although Kit had come to terms with the move from California, she made a habit of not watching *New Jersey News*. It seemed the right moment to change her ways.

When she sat up, the mattress shifted, and poor Sam the Baby thrashed desperately, as if he felt himself falling. "Oh, Sam!" She picked up the sweet perfect little guy, resting his little chin on her shoulder, and Sam threw up everything in his tiny tummy.

Curdled hot stinking milk ran down her back and soaked through her shirt. "Sam!" She held him up in the air, her two hands straddling his back. His eyes opened all the way, and he seemed to spot her and consider the meaning of this huge set of hands and this huge face.

There was a large circular wet spot on her bedspread.

"Sam!"

She undid his diaper. It was completely

dry. "Okay, I'm catching on. I didn't tighten it enough. When you peed, it ran out the side." She yanked off her own filthy shirt, washed her back, put on a new shirt, and mopped the baby up with a warm damp washcloth.

New Jersey News began.

A little box in the corner of the screen said 6:01 P.M. Dusty had left a newborn baby with her ex-stepdaughter for three hours.

The baby began to cry. This was real. Not a whimper. He was a very little guy, very new to this world, but he could announce his problems a lot louder than a new kitten could announce its problems. Kit had no idea how to comfort him or quiet him. If being dry didn't help, and being fed didn't help, and being cuddled didn't help — what were your other options?

"Don't cry like that," suggested Kit.

Newark schools were having financial difficulties.

"Ssshhhh!" she said. "Be a nice guy, Sam."

A power plant was having minor but meaningful failures.

She, too, was having a failure. She hoped it was minor. How did you know with babies whether you were in big trouble or little trouble? Sam began to turn red from shrieking. She patted his back. She rubbed his tummy. She kissed his forehead.

He was not soothed.

A state representative was resigning under mysterious circumstances. State police were closer to solving a rash of ATM crimes.

The baby's yelling dwindled. He gave her a sad look and threw up on her again.

The weather was to continue fair and seasonably warm. Stocks were up.

At least she knew if there had been a kidnapping, it had not been reported to *NJN*.

"Dusty," she said out loud, "you'd better come back here fast, or I'm going to do something."

Yeah? she said to herself. Like what?

The baby slept, or else slid into a coma. She could not see his tiny chest lift, nor hear air drawn into his lungs. What if something was wrong?

The phone rang.

Kit was so startled by the ring she quivered like the baby, halfway to shudders. She rushed to grab it, so a second ring wouldn't startle the baby. "Dusty!" she shouted. "You better get back here! I am so mad at you! What am I supposed to do with the baby?"

There was no answer.

No sound at all.

Very gently the caller hung up.

It was Ed Bing, she thought.

No, if it was Ed Bing he'd talk to me. He'd say, How come you pretended you hadn't seen Dusty in months?

So who was it?

A telemarketer?

A wrong number?

She was abruptly, completely afraid. Swallowed, immersed, drowning in fear.

She could hardly hoist Sam, she was shaking so badly.

I'm going home before I suffocate, she decided. Dusty expects me to be here, but when she finally arrives and I'm not here, surely even Dusty will know to go to Mom's house instead.

Kit flung the baby's things into a school backpack that hung on her closet door, wrapped the blanket around the baby, and went downstairs. Slowly, even though she wanted to race, because she had never carried this kind of burden before. She didn't take the carrier; she was walking home. She would not go by the road. Ed Bing and his awful long low derelict car were out on those roads. She would slip along the edge of the golf course, and it would be safe and beautiful, with sunlight and green grass and golfers choosing their clubs.

The doorbell rang.

Ed.

She was shocked by her weakness. With an infant in her arms, she could not fight, use a phone, run, blockade — anything! The presence of the baby rendered her helpless. Faced with an opponent, she could only hunch her shoulders over the infant and hope for mercy.

This time she peeked through the view hole high in the center of the front door.

It was Row, with his little sister.

Chapter 5

Rowen Mason had driven around, and he and Muffin had had an ice-cream cone and stopped to look at new sports cars at three dealerships, while Muffin whined and complained and wanted to go back to Aunt Karen's and see the movies after all and be friends. By now Rowen had forgotten what his fight with Shea had been about, and Muffin had not known in the first place, and Row called Shea to see if Kit had arrived yet, and Shea said, No, and furthermore she wasn't home, and her parents weren't home, and earlier today Kit had been headed for her dad's empty house to pick up some clothes, and why didn't Row drive over there and round her up and bring her on over so they could decide which pizzas to order.

Rowen liked this assignment, which allowed him to get Kit without looking as if he'd chosen to come get Kit. He even liked having his baby sister there as backup, and even admitted it to himself.

It did not look as if anybody was home. The place had that vacant expression common to Seven Hills, every house just plunked down, not attached to the ground yet; they needed fences and shrubs and old swing sets to look permanent. But while the windows of other houses exhibited neatly tied drapes or hanging bits of lace, Mr. Innes's house looked sealed, every drape drawn tight, nothing showing but the plain vanilla linings.

Kit, like Rowen, dressed well. That made them exceptions in school. Kit had her share of torn jeans, sagging pants, old T-shirts, and ripped sweats, and she did wear them, but more often, she wore exactly what Rowen wore: catalog clothing. Beautifully put-together clothes crying out for photographers and a spot on page three.

It came to him that he and Kit even had the same haircut; but Row's hair clung to his head, thin and silky, while Kit's puffed around her head, thick and generous. She wore tiny earrings, no shape or meaning to them, just a dot of sparkle.

They were both in marching band, and he had been there while she tried on band uniforms. Everybody looked splendid in band uniforms — white creased pants, scarlet jacket, gold buttons, and shoulder fringe. Kit played flute, along with about thirty other girls. Flute was a girl instrument. He himself was a drummer and, in Row's opinion, the other instruments were just there for looks. Across a football field, you could hear the percussion, and a whiff of brass, but you never heard the flutes except maybe a piccolo.

Shea played piccolo. Hers was the shrill scream of notes that rose above everything. People who played piccolo had no fears.

He loved marching band. The swoop and maneuver of the band on the field was so beautiful. Wind might whisk away the sound of the trumpets and the trombones from half the field, but it could not take away the gleaming beauty of the horns.

He thought maybe he and Kit could start with a band conversation, talk about the new pattern they were learning, the new conductor they weren't so sure of, the upcoming schedule, the bus they'd take. He was surprised by how worried he was over talking with Kit. It had suddenly assumed huge proportions, as if on this speech hung his future and his hopes.

The door opened. Kit was not holding a flute, but a squalling, screaming, quivering red-faced baby.

All speech was driven from his mind and mouth.

"I wish I had a hand free to photograph you, Row," Kit told him, "because your expression is priceless."

"Where's the camera?" said Muffin. "I'll take his picture."

"Too late," said Row. "I'm no longer surprised." But he was. What was Kit doing here with a little teeny baby? Wasn't Kit his cousin's best friend? Wouldn't Shea have mentioned it if there was a new baby at Kit's house? Whose new baby? Wasn't her father on the West Coast? Anyway, weren't they pretty old for having babies?

He finally looked at Kit again, and she said, "Oh, Row! I am so glad to see you. I have had the strangest afternoon." She gave him a sweet smile and he fell into it. It was that smile that had drawn Row, because she seemed like a person who meant to smile a lot more than she did. She was too serious.

Kit let them in and they automatically moved to the back of the house. The front rooms were so formal, so much the property of the decorator, that nobody could imagine actually bothering with those rooms. They flung themselves down on a vast green leather sofa. Rowen had never seen such large furniture. There was so much to look at. Kit. The inexplicable baby. The house, which seemed so un-homey for a girl like Kit.

Kit couldn't remember the little sister's name. It was a silly nickname, she thought, something that would be embarrassing once the kid was older. But she couldn't bring it to mind.

"Can I hold the baby?" said the little sister eagerly. She was a cute little thing, stick thin, as if her wrists would not be equal to the weight of the baby.

"No, Muffin," said Rowen sharply, "you can't. You don't know how to hold babies."

Muffin. I knew it was something pathetic, thought Kit. "I haven't had any practice at holding babies, either," she told Muffin. "Today is my first day ever. Come on, between us we'll figure out how you can hold the baby."

Muffin sat down on the immense couch and eased herself back and back some more until her legs stuck straight out in front of her. She had plenty of lap now. Kit gently maneuvered the baby into Muffin's arms, and Muffin sagged joyfully back on the couch and smiled down at him. Her smile transformed her. She was suddenly, beautifully, a mommy in training, like a Halloween costume.

Kit beamed at Muffin.

She had to have a photograph of this. She would make extra copies, because Row and Muffin's mother would certainly want one. She found the camera she'd used to photograph Sam the Baby and Ed the Creepy Cousin and took two angles of Muffin and Sam. Then she took a photo of Row looking puzzled, and a final shot of Row looking irritated.

"Enough with the immortality, Kit. We came to collect you for movies," said Rowen. "But I don't think they're newborn-rated."

They all laughed.

"He seems really little," Rowen said. Is he okay? Is he meant to be that small?" Rowen took the disposable camera from Kit, knelt next to his sister, and took a shot of Muffin's cheek resting against Sam's.

Kit loved how they were with each other. How sweet when a big brother was that fond of a little sister. Her throat choked up a little. Was she, at this very moment, a big sister?

"I don't know, Rowen," she said. "I was on my way home to wait for my mother to get back from shopping when you and Muffin came to the door. I figured I'd hand the baby to Mom, and she would know things like whether the baby is too small."

Rowen stared at Kit. Really stared. "Who's the mother of this baby, then?" Even his voice stared at her. "Whose baby is this? What's going on?" He pulled back from Kit in every way, as if he did not know her after all.

Kit had been soothed by their company and the silly posing for photographs, but now she realized that Row was reacting the way he ought to — and she, Kit, had not reacted the way she should have. She'd let herself drift around, like Dusty, whose porch light was definitely not on.

A baby abandoned on the doorstep was not puzzling.

It was shocking.

Muffin was awestruck.

How incredible that this little soft folded-up thing with its little elbows and knees curled like bananas was a person! It seemed as if it might be something else entirely.

It had perfect, incredibly tiny fingers, with perfect tiny fingernails and perfect tiny knuckles. Its little sweet eyes tried to find hers but couldn't, so Muffin shifted herself until she was in front of the eyes, and the baby smiled at her.

She feasted her eyes on the beautiful infant. Row and Kit were talking, but Muffin paid no attention; how could she think of anything except this baby? "What's his name?" she interrupted them.

"I don't know his name," said Kit. "I made one up. I'm calling him Sam the Baby."

Sam the Baby.

It sounded like one of Muffin's favorite picture books from when she was very small, where they combined silly stories and counting and ridiculous made-up animals. Red fish, two fish, Sam wish, ham wich. "Hello, Sam the Baby," she said very softly, and she put her lips on his cheek and it was the softest, most perfect thing she had ever touched and then she yelled, "Peeeee — you!"

"He does need his diaper changed," agreed Kit. She was laughing. "I did just the same thing, Muff. I was thinking how sweet and adorable he was, and then I smelled him."

"He doesn't even notice," said Muffin. "How can he live inside himself when he stinks like that?"

She helped Kit change the baby and this, too, was amazing, because the baby did not know that he was bare, and being held, and being washed, whereas if Muffin were being treated this way she would die of humiliation and hide under blankets.

He doesn't know anything yet, thought Muffin, and this filled her with awe, and with kinship; as if Sam were her brother. There was so much Muffin didn't know yet, either, and it tired her out, staring at the years of school in which she must learn, learn, learn; catch up, catch up, catch up; remember, remember, remember. And Sam didn't even know that yet. He was just here, and now he didn't smell anymore, and she loved him for knowing nothing.

Row said, in a heavy, almost angry voice that made Muffin watch him hard, "Kit. What is going on? Of course you know the baby's real name. You're his baby-sitter."

"Or possibly his sister," said Kit.

"You're supposed to be sure of things like that."

"It hasn't been that kind of day," said Kit, and she told them what had happened since three o'clock.

"It sounds like a typical Dusty screwup," said Rowen at last. "I remember when your dad married her. No offense, but my parents said he was totally nuts and the marriage wouldn't last half an hour. Dusty really and truly has a room temperature IQ. What do you bet that she went and had this baby, and then the day she came home from the hospital, she got kicked out of her apartment for some Dusty-type reason, like having friends over to line-dance at three in the morning when tired old ladies who need their sleep are living on the floor beneath her? So she drove over here to live."

Kit thought about Rowen's explanation. It was entirely possible that Dusty had come here to camp out.

"Why didn't you just ask Dusty?" said Muffin. "I don't think you handled this well, Kit. I think my mother would say that you —"

"Muff!" said Rowen.

"Dusty didn't give me time," said Kit, "but you're right about what your mother would say. Probably the same thing my mother would say. But Dusty is the mother this time! It's so like Dusty to be stupid, and drive around, and hurl her most precious possession into somebody else's care while she races off with what nobody else would call a strategy."

"He's falling asleep," whispered Muffin. "Stop talking."

"I don't think he'll notice if we keep talking," said Kit.

"Did you see his eyes close?" said Rowen. "They just clamped shut."

They admired the baby for a while. Sleeping babies, Kit realized, were perfect, whereas waking babies had drawbacks.

"Maybe Dusty's blackmailing your father," said Rowen, "because it is your father's baby and she's going to make him pay."

Kit shook her head. "Blackmail is out. Dad's a wonderful father and if he's the father of this baby, he'd be a good one. But I'm sure he's not. Dusty wanted to stay with him. If they were having a baby, she'd have told him in order to get him back, and it would have worked. So it isn't blackmail and Sam isn't his."

She hadn't stopped to think that of course Dusty would tell Dad; it was interesting how talking out loud was a way to hear yourself. She felt a pang of sorrow, though, because then Sam wasn't hers, either. She imagined Sam growing up somewhere unknown to her, becoming a kid and a teenager and a man, and she would never know. She had only this afternoon. Suddenly, weirdly, she was grateful to Dusty for giving her this strange afternoon. Her only day with Sam the Baby.

"Kidnapping, then," said Rowen.

"It wasn't on *NJN*."

"Dusty ordered them to keep it quiet or she wouldn't give the baby back after they paid her the ransom."

"Be real, Rowen. Dusty can't plan a run to the grocery."

"Stupid people commit the most crimes," said Rowen. "They don't notice the pitfalls that smarter people would notice."

"Row heard that on TV," said Muffin. "He's quoting a cop show."

In Muffin's arms, the baby had slumped into what looked like a very uncomfortable posture, but perhaps babies didn't know about comfort yet. He had fallen into a sort of stupor, staring wide-eyed at nothing.

"So you have no idea what to do next?" asked Muffin. "I know, though. I always know what to do next. Listen to me. We'll take him home with us. My mother loves babies."

"Muff," said Rowen — in the kind of voice that meant Shut up or I'll squash you — and the phone rang again.

"This time," said Kit, "it has to be Dusty. I'm counting on it to be Dusty." She picked up the phone.

"But be more sensible," said Rowen. "Don't give anything away."

So Kit said carefully, "Hello?"

"Hi, is this Kit Innes?" said a woman's voice. It was a pleasant and friendly voice, but not familiar to Kit. Not Dad's assistant, not his secretary, not his travel agent.

"Yes," she said uncertainly.

Row stood up and came close to listen in on the phone. She held it a little away from her ear so he could follow the conversation.

But he was very close to her, and it distracted Kit. She thought of his shirt, and of Row under it; and she thought of how worried she had been about how to talk to him, but they had had the topic of the year, as it happened, and subjects were not going to be a problem. Her eyes met his and she felt a flutter intense enough that she had to turn her whole face away in order to hear the woman on the line.

"This is Cinda Chance," said the woman. "I'm another cousin of Ed and Dusty's. I am so relieved to have reached you, Kit.

We are so desperately worried about both Dusty and the baby. I know you were shaken by Ed coming over, and I apologize for that. We're at our wits' end, you see. My husband, Burt, and I are adopting Dusty's baby, you know, and we're so excited, we've been waiting for years for this to happen, and now Dusty is worried about her decision, and we're trying to be understanding, but Dusty just flew off in her car without anyplace to go. And that's like Dusty, you know, that didn't surprise us, but we're so worried about the baby. Is the baby all right? That's all that really matters right now."

What a relief! What a sensible easy explanation. And how like Dusty. "Oh, Cinda, I am so glad you called. You almost missed me. I was just going home to ask my mother what to do."

"No, don't bring your parents into this," said Cinda. "Really, we have it all under control. Is the baby all right?" Her voice was high and urgent.

"Oh, he's fine," Kit promised, "he's just fine. I've fed him, and changed him, and we're cuddling him on the couch, and he's just fine. You're going to love him. Have you met him yet?"

"We? Who's we?" said Cinda.

Kit did not feel like long explanations. "Two of my friends are over here helping me with him," said Kit.

Muffin beamed. Kit had won an admirer.

Cinda said, "Kit, I also have to apologize because Ed told me he scouted around the house and peered in windows and scared you. He shouldn't have done that. It's just that we were both coming apart, worrying if Dusty would take good care of the baby."

They had been right to worry. Dusty had not taken care of the baby. She had not even told Kit how to take care of the baby before abandoning him. But Sam was not abandoned. He had a family waiting. Cousins. And they weren't Ed, and they were nice.

"I just feel so much better hearing your voice," said Kit. "You sound just right for a mother."

Row muttered, "Not so fast, Kit. You don't have any idea who that is. And she didn't say whether she'd met the baby, she just wanted to know who's here with you."

Kit glared at him. "She's just upset!" she hissed. "She's had a terrible day of worry." Rowen had no idea what it was like to wait for an adoption baby to arrive. Kit knew, because she had read lots of articles in women's magazines and listened to several panels on talk shows. You and your husband had to go through examinations and inquisitions and inspections, and it took weeks and months to qualify for a baby, but then there was no baby available, and you had to wait and wait and wait and wait, and then when you found out there was going to be a baby, and it would be born in — say, September, like Sam — then you bought all the baby things, and told all your friends, and took time off from work, and practiced changing diapers — and the mother — say, Dusty — changed her mind.

No wonder Ed had been crazy! Kit would have run over a flower bed, too, if she had been waiting for Sam all her life and couldn't find him, didn't know if he was all right. Well, of course, it wasn't Ed waiting for the baby, it was Cinda and Burt Chance. What nice names! The baby was going to be Sam Chance. No, that didn't really work. She would have to ask what name the baby was really and truly going to have. Jonathan Chance. Alexander Chance. Michael William Chance. There were lots of wonderful possibilities.

"Kit, would you be a darling and bring the baby to us?" said Cinda. "Ed is driving everywhere he can think of to find the baby, hoping to find Dusty at one of her old haunts, and Burt is driving everywhere *he* can think of. I have to stay by the phone, and we so badly, badly want our baby here and we want him now." Her voice broke with grief, and Kit's heart exploded for her. Kit was the one cuddling and kissing this perfect little guy while his mommy, his mommy who had waited for years and years, was alone in the house with a phone!

Kit did have a driver's license, and Dad had given her a car for her sixteenth birthday. It was in the garage at home. It was an ugly square Volvo. She hated the looks of it, but Dad felt she would be safer in it than any other vehicle. So she was safe, though totally not cool. On the other hand, it was probably the best car for hauling a baby in. And the car carrier was upstairs.

Rowen said very quietly, "You were afraid of Ed Bing."

"Row, this is the baby's mother."

"No, she isn't. She wants to be the baby's mother."

"But that's wonderful, Row! She's waiting for him! Do you see Dusty waiting for the baby? Cinda's probably been choosing names for the whole nine months, and Dusty hasn't even picked one out yet. A cousin is a just right person to adopt a baby."

"I don't see how being a cousin qualifies you for anything," said Rowen. "You've never laid eyes on this Cinda. How do you know she's a cousin? Just because she says so?"

It was true that Ed had come alone to the wedding. Kit could not remember other relatives on Dusty's side. But who would claim to be related to Dusty unless they were? And it was a relief to know that Dusty could do something right: She could admit that her cousins would be better parents than she would. It was only natural to have a few worries at the last moment. If Dusty had been here at Dad's house, Dusty would decide, but the day was ending, night was coming, and this baby needed a parent and one was on the phone. It sounded perfect to Kit.

"Let's go ask your mother," said Row in an interfering pushy way. "Or Shea's mother. Or mine."

She had been so glad to see Row, and now she was just irked. He was getting in the way. He was all inconvenient advice and obstruction.

"Or the police," said Rowen.

Kit's hand was over the phone to muffle

their conversation. She glared at him.

"Do you think we should call 911?" said Muffin intently.

"No!" said Kit. "We are not facing an emergency. And I don't want Dusty in trouble. I don't want some social worker taking poor Sam the Baby and sticking him in a foster home for months until they decide what to do next. I want Sam the Baby to be home in his own crib tonight."

Cinda said, "I'm sorry, Kit, I can't quite hear what you're saying. Please, Kit, please, I need your help and I need it now."

"Ask her where Dusty is," hissed Rowen.

Muffin hissed right back, "Row!"

"They don't know where Dusty is," Kit told him irritably. "Yes, Cinda," she said, "I can take the baby to your house."

"Can I go, too?" cried Muffin. "I'm a great baby-sitter. I love Sam the Baby. I'll come and I'll help. You'll need help."

"*Muff,*" said Rowen.

But Kit said, "Yes, you can come. I'll be glad to have the company, and if you're in the backseat with him I won't be looking back every second to see if he's all right and then maybe having a fatal, Dusty-type accident when I'm not looking at the road." Kit hoped Row would want to come, too.

Or do the driving himself, in the car he handily had in the driveway.

The directions Cinda gave were long. Kit read them back into the phone to be sure she had the right turns and route numbers and landmarks, and Rowen said, "Those guys are seriously hiding from their fellow man."

"Would you like to come, Row?" Kit asked nervously. She didn't know how she felt toward Rowen right now. He was being a jerk, trying to make the decision about the baby, but she would certainly like to have his company. She felt muddled. It was as if Dusty had climbed into her brain.

"I don't think you should do this," said Rowen flatly, "and I don't want to get mixed up in it."

"So you won't come?" Kit snapped.

"You shouldn't go, either," he said. "Just do me a favor. Just call your mother and ask what she thinks."

But Mom wasn't home. They'd have to wait for Mom to show up, and then Mom would come over, and they would have to discuss things, one of which would be: Why didn't you tell me about this in the first place? Mom would insist on waiting for

Dusty, and even more time would pass, and authorities would be brought in, and Dusty would be in trouble, because Dusty was always in trouble, and Dad would be crazed that he had to deal with her again, and he would stay on his coast and not come to Kit's, and he'd hold Kit half responsible. And meanwhile, where would Sam the Baby sleep, and would Cinda and Burt, the cousins, be able to take him?

Kit wanted to drive in the driveway with the new baby and be the one to place the baby in its mother's arms.

She loved this picture, and reminded herself to take along a camera or two, because Cinda and Burt Chance would have bought their baby album, and now she, Kit, would take the first roll of film to fill it. What a gift!

Muffin could hardly believe that Rowen agreed to let her go along. Probably he thought it would be easier to explain to Mom and Dad than violent movies. Or maybe he was assuming he wouldn't have to explain anything to Mom and Dad, and that was probably right, because Kit and Muffin and Sam the Baby would meet the new parents and then Kit and Muffin would drive back to Shea's and none of their own parents would ever know anything about it.

Muffin tucked the disposable camera into the little front kangaroo pocket of her own pink sweatshirt.

She would take pictures of the new mommy and daddy meeting their new baby.

Kit brought the baby carrier downstairs. It seemed designed for a larger person, who would sit up and take notice. Sam the Baby just folded into a ball and slept in his carrier the way Muffin slept in her kangaroo bag.

"Why didn't the baby's new parents come to the hospital?" asked Muffin. In second grade, the teacher had read out loud a book about adoption. It was beautiful. But Muffin didn't know anybody who was adopted. Now she did. Sam.

"I guess there was a mix-up," said Kit.

Muffin hated this kind of answer. That was the trouble with being nine. People knew so much more than you did. What kind of mix-up? Muffin felt grumpy. Then she looked at Sam.

When you were nine, it was crummy to

know nothing, but when you were new, like Sam, it was awesome and miraculous.

"I would love to have you for a brother, Sam the baby," whispered Muffin. "I could be the older one, instead of Rowen always being the older one. And you would think I knew everything, instead of Rowen always telling me I know nothing. And I would make my mother change you, because you're too disgusting for me. I would take care of you when you were clean and beautiful."

Sam the Baby opened his eyes, which were very large for his face, while his nose was way too small, just a perky spot in the middle of his stare. He blinked his eyes, and long dark lashes swept his cheeks, and Muffin laughed at him, and she thought, His lucky, lucky mommy and daddy.

She could hardly wait to meet them, the way she loved to meet all her friends' parents, because the dads would pick you up and pull on your ponytail, and the moms would listen to your stories and fix you snacks and fix your hair, and they remembered what vegetable you had not wanted to eat last time.

She hoped, and it was treason, that Sam the Baby's new mommy and daddy liked all food, the way Aunt Karen and Uncle Anthony did, instead of no food, like Mom.

Kit seemed to have lost the camera she'd been using, which was annoying, but that was how disposable cameras were. They disappeared for months, but eventually turned up and the pictures were developed, and you had the additional treat of photos from a forgotten occasion.

Kit got another camera from the stack while Rowen hefted the carrier out to his car, so he could drive Kit to her car. Sam noticed nothing. He went right on snoozing even as they shifted his little body. He won't know who changes him, thought Kit, or who loves him, or who his mother is, or who adopts him.

It was a strange, even terrifying thought: Sam the Baby had no thoughts about the things that were happening to him.

She took six photographs immediately, in case she never found the other camera, so that she would still have a memory of Sam to keep.

Rowen drove them to Kit's house. Mom's sporty red Miata and Malcolm's heavy champagne BMW were not there. It was strange to think of all this happening and no parents knew.

Rowen transferred the carrier to Kit's car.

"Where's Shea, anyway?" asked Kit as she strapped herself into the driver's seat of the Volvo and Muffin found a place in the back next to Sam.

"We had a big fight," said Row, without the slightest interest in Shea or the fight. When you were cousins you could be casual like that. "She didn't like the movies I picked out and said I was a slime and why didn't I leave and I said I was not a slime —"

"He is a slime," Muffin explained.

"— and Shea threw us out —"

"Call Shea back," said Kit, "and tell her as soon as Muffin and I have delivered Sam the Baby, we will be there for movies and spending the night. Don't eat all the food without us."

Chapter 6

Route 80 West.

It was a good thing Kit had plenty of gas. Cinda had given her the exit number, but she hadn't said it was fifteen miles! Oh, well. At seventy miles an hour, which was the scary rate traffic was moving, it didn't take long. Kit, who was new to driving, preferred speeds like thirty miles an hour.

It was a relief to get off the highway.

North on Dexter Mill Road. They were practically in Pennsylvania.

It was beautiful, hilly country. The leaves had just begun turning. Splashes and trills of scarlet and orange leaves flared in the sunset and then vanished. The sky deepened quickly from blue to slate.

In the backseat, Muffin sang songs she

remembered from her own babyhood, not so long ago. "Ride a pretty little horsey," she sang to Sam.

At a twenty-four-hour convenience store (convenient to whom? There were no houses!) Kit turned left on Hennicot Road. Hennicot Road was just there; it seemed to serve no houses, no schools, no stores, no population whatsoever. It seemed not to go anywhere except farther and farther away. Muffin's earlier question, the one Kit had answered so casually, sprang back into her mind. Why hadn't the new parents come to the hospital?

Kit had not done much driving in the dark, but then, where she lived, it never really got dark. Every road — and her part of the state was a solid interweaving of roads — was lined with streetlights, and every store stayed open late, glowing with light, so darkness was only an occasional pocket.

Here, the trees closed overhead and the road tunneled beneath them, and she no longer knew what the sky was doing. Hennicot Road had potholes. Not ordinary potholes from the weight of trucks and the convulsions of freezing weather. Old crumbling holes, as if so few people drove here there was no reason to repave.

Kit had never been any place that was not full of people.

The huge sprawl that was New York City, that extended deep into New Jersey, had vanished. She was in a country she did not know; had not known existed. They went past the kind of house where people married their relatives, and had snarly foxy dogs that bit, and used the insides of cars for porch chairs.

"Aaaaahhhhhh, Kit!" shrieked Muffin.

Kit's fingers went into spasm on the wheel.

"He's going to the bathroom all over the place. He stinks! He's worse than the oil tank farms on the New Jersey Turnpike! You have to change him. Drive over there to that diner. We'll use their restroom to wash up in."

He did stink. His smell slowly filled the Volvo.

Muffin was right about the diner. Lenore's Breakfast and Lunch, it said. Kit was sorry Lenore didn't serve dinner. She needed human beings. She would have gone in and ordered anything, just to be among people. Gratefully, Kit pulled into the parking lot. When she turned off the motor, she realized the diner was boarded up.

Plywood nailed over windows had split with age. Long peels of wooden layers hung at angles. A padlock on the front door hung open. An abandoned Dumpster overflowed with trash. Weeds grew up through the gravel, and vines were lifting the shingles from the roof of the diner.

Muffin climbed into the front seat. "He's icky," she said. "I'm not touching anybody icky."

"Some baby-sitter you are," said Kit.

The silence of the car and the silence outside the car was too much. Kit turned the ignition, got the radio again, and clicked the all-door lock. Then she got herself out of her seat belt, hauled herself to her knees, and leaned way over the seat back to examine the damage Sam the Baby had wrought. "Oh, for a pair of gloves," she said. He had diarrhea all the way up his little back and halfway down his little legs. He smelled like a family of skunks.

Holding her breath, vowing that she herself would have babies who were neat and careful about this kind of thing, she had to use about ten of the baby wipes Dusty had tucked into the carrier. Now, what was she supposed to do with his disgusting clothes, his very used diaper, and all these revolting baby wipes?

She wrapped all of it up in one of his two blankets and looked out into the darkness. The entire property was one big garbage can. Kit, who recycled all things at all times, hurled her disgusting bundle into the chaos of old televisions, beer cans, and car parts. Then she rolled the window back up and turned on the heater to dry the baby's clean bare body. Kit could not help bending forward and kissing his round tummy. She had not known that the nakedness of babies, the perfection of their little bodies, was so beautiful.

"Stay asleep, Sam," she whispered. His breathing continued uninterrupted. He didn't know she was talking to him. He knew nothing but the inside of his sleepy little world. He felt safe enough to sleep. He trusted her with his little self.

He trusts me, thought Kit.

He had put his little life into her arms. All his world was her choice. Either she would take good care of him — or she would not.

Oh, Sam the Baby! thought Kit. Do you realize what you've done? You've made me your mother, or sitter, or sister. If I could choose, which would I be? I don't want to be anybody's mother yet. I've never liked baby-sitting. That leaves sister. *What if you are my brother?* I'll be giving up my own brother to a pack of strangers.

I should have called Dad. I should have gone home and waited for Mom to get back from shopping, like Row said. Or maybe even called Malcolm. I can't even tell if I'm taking good care of you, Sam. You look fine, but was that kind of diarrhea fine? And this is the last diaper in the package.

She wrapped him, bare except for his diaper, inside the remaining blanket, tucking the end in until he was a papoose: no arms, no legs, just his shining face.

She ordered Muffin to get in back with him.

"What if he gets stinky again?" said Muffin.

"Impossible. There's nothing left inside him." She scrubbed her hands with the last baby wipe and set off. Over and over, she muttered the directions. "Right on Swamp Maple."

This whole day was a swamp. Where were these people? Where on earth did Cinda and Burt live? And why? There was no other traffic. In this very heavily populated state, hers was the only car on the road.

Swamp Maple wound among hills and through woods and next to silent still ponds.

At one-point-six miles, Cinda had said, on the left, you'll see a broken white picket fence. Turn left and go down the drive in the center of the fence.

There was the fence, white, and very broken.

The fence pickets were sharply pointed like toothpicks, whole sections smashed as if some angry person had driven right through. Her headlights caught trees strangled by wild grapevines, and in one place the vines had hoisted a piece of broken fence into the air.

"This," said Muffin, "is the spookiest place I've ever been in my life."

Kit stopped in the middle of the road, staring at the driveway to Burt and Cinda's. There weren't many places in the state of New Jersey where you could stop in the middle of the road and not worry about horns blaring in your ears and cars ripping past you because you were delaying them five seconds.

"The woods are going to eat us," said Muffin.

"Don't be silly," said Kit. "Probably when we get to their house, it'll be this beautiful mansion with horses in a green field. This is Burt and Cinda's weekend home, where they come for peace and quiet."

Kit turned into the lane. She'd never driven on gravel and it seemed to talk under her tires, arguing with her. Little stones spit out the sides. The woods were dark, viney, and wet. She would have turned around, except the road was so narrow, there was no way to turn around. She hardly knew how to back up. She only went places where she could go forward.

"Or maybe," said Muffin, "they're witches and this is their coven."

And now the gravel and the woods ended and became meadow, and it turned out that the sun had not finished setting, but just vanished behind the thickness of forest. A great swath of purple and rose sky welcomed them.

Silhouetted against the sky was a sweet little cottage with shutters at the windows, flowers in beds, and cars parked in the driveway. The drive made a little oval, so Kit was automatically facing home again and did not have to panic over how she was going to turn around.

Already people were bursting out of the house. Three people — two men and a woman — the woman way ahead of the men.

The woman had to be Cinda.

Cinda was thin in a lean strong way, as if she spent her life running toward something. She was maybe thirty. She wore a plain gray T-shirt, hanging down over khaki pants. She had chosen large black-rimmed glasses, as if her dream were to be mistaken for a computer geek. Cinda was pumped. It made Kit smile to see her. Kit adored Sam the Baby, and now here was his mommy, come to snuggle and hug for the very first time.

And yet . . . and yet . . .

Ed was chugging behind Cinda, and in the settling dusk he looked more civilized; his pockmarks didn't show, nor his yellow gnarly hands. Had Kit misjudged him?

Behind them, walking slowly, almost dragging, came another man, who must be Burt. He wore blue jeans so new and starchy-looking they'd probably stand up on their own, but his pullover sweater was misshapen and the neckline was unraveling. He did not smile but glanced twice at his watch, and when he drew up to the car, it was not the baby he looked at, nor his wife, nor Kit, but Ed Bing.

Cinda was tugging at the back door to

get her hands on Sam, but all four doors were locked.

Cinda and Ed, but not Burt, stooped to look inside the Volvo, peering and squinting, and again Ed cupped his hands to see better, and his eyes surrounded by his fat fists were red and glaring. Kit clicked the locks undone, and Cinda opened the back door.

Row tuned the radio to an all-news-all-the-time station. There had been every kind of crime, from the new ATM scam to the old drunk driving tragedy. But no kidnapping.

He was ill with worry.

This had never happened to him before. Even the night before his SATs, even the hour before his first varsity game, he had not felt this sick roiling in his gut.

At first he thought he might actually be sick, and Mom would expect him to go home, take an aspirin, and go to bed early. But if there was one thing Row hated more than being sick, it was giving in to being sick. All his life, he'd hated going to bed.

What were his choices, here, now that he'd let Kit and Muffin drive away without him? He could go to Shea's and twiddle around, waiting to see if they got back safely. But this would involve explanations to Aunt Karen and Uncle Anthony, and although his aunt and uncle seemed flaky to strangers, it was a facade. Messy, noisy, chaotic, and wacky — but they were very very careful of their children. Shea, who was the youngest — her two brothers were in college — did not do anything without supervision.

He, Rowen Mason, age sixteen, with an IQ many points above Dusty's had been just as much of a jerk.

He had let Kit drive off into the unknown — *truly* unknown! He himself had said that these people are seriously hiding from their fellow humans — and he'd let his nine-year-old sister go along! All they knew of Cinda, Burt, and Ed was that Kit was afraid of Ed, and Ed expressed himself by driving over flower beds.

Rowen comforted himself with the fact that Ed Bing really was Dusty's cousin. Therefore the whole thing had a certain in-the-family safety net. But why had Dusty disappeared? Why hadn't the adopting parents gotten the baby at the hospital? Had Dusty changed her mind about giving up Sam the Baby? She had certainly made up her mind fast enough when she had a chance to give the baby to Kit.

Rowen had not even wanted to touch the baby. It was too little. It didn't look like babies in ads for tires or insurance. It looked all red and sunken. Even its little sob was scrawny. Had *he* ever been that little?

And when he was, had Mom and Dad tossed him here and there, driving away, forgetting to tell people his name?

Mom and Dad were out.

But Aunt Karen and Uncle Anthony were home.

He wanted to ask them what they thought, but he knew what they would think. They would be furious and appalled. They would not even waste time yelling at him. They might actually call the police. He might have to admit to the police that yes, his nine-year-old sister, an unknown baby, and a teenage friend of his had driven off into the back of beyond because of one phone call from a strange voice. And he, Row, had said huffily, you're being dumb — and then let them do it. He should have insisted on an adult's advice before Kit took off, and if Kit wouldn't change her mind, he should have gone, too.

He had had them all in his own car, and

he could have done the driving, or simply driven to a better destination — Aunt Karen and Uncle Anthony's.

He changed radio stations, hoping to be distracted by some decent music. But it was news hour everywhere. The ATM scam was big stuff; events were unfolding at this very moment. Police were expecting to make arrests shortly. Things, said the spokeswoman importantly, were happening fast.

If something happens, thought Row, and I'm not there . . .

But what could happen?

What was he afraid of?

He drove aimlessly.

Usually Rowen found this totally satisfying, exploring every road, testing every intersection. Now he circled near Kit's father's house, trying to remember the directions Cinda had given over the phone. Route 80 West — and then what?

Route 80 went all the way to California.

Muffin was pleased with the new family.

The house was the kind that would be full of happy dogs and sleeping cats and stuffed teddy bears and baskets of rose petals. There would be a refrigerator jammed with nibbly things; and the new mommy would want them to sit down and have something yummy to eat and get to know the baby together and talk about everything, but none of this mattered.

What mattered was that Muffin needed to go to the bathroom.

Bad.

Cinda was clapping and opening the door. "Oh, here's my baby! Here is my baby! Oh, he's so beautiful, he's so perfect!" She leaned over Muffin without even seeing her. She undid Sam's straps and lifted him across Muffin's lap and out of the car and up onto her shoulder, still laughing, and now kissing as well.

Muffin had forgotten to get her camera ready, but Kit had not. That was another nice thing about being older; you didn't forget stuff. You paid attention. Muffin reminded herself to pay attention.

Kit focused the gaudy yellow box on Cinda's face and caught a perfect picture of a mommy's coo when she first saw her son. Muffin was happy. There was nothing Muffin liked better than sitting on Gramma's lap and looking at Muffin's own baby books.

Cinda jounced Sam the Baby — a little too hard for Muffin's taste. On the other hand, Muffin really had to go to the bathroom and all bouncing was a threat.

"Look!" Cinda cried to the men. "Look! My baby."

Kit had gotten out of the car and was aiming across the car roof, taking photographs of the entire family.

Muffin clambered out, thinking of bathrooms and how many seconds she had left before she had an accident.

One man was scary, his face all pocked up and a cigarette dangling from his lips. Mom, who was into healthy, would be crazed that this new baby was going into a smoking family. The man probably only smokes outside, Muffin comforted herself.

The other man was thin and small. Muffin hoped she wouldn't grow up to look as not grown-up as this guy. He was having trouble with his watchband or something, and did not glance at Sam or Cinda.

Muffin's camera was still in the little two-handed front pocket of her sweatshirt, but she didn't need it, with Kit taking all those pictures. She needed a bathroom. Muffin scooted around the cluster of grown-ups and baby.

The garage swung sideways off the house and there was a door between the garage and the house. That was probably the mudroom, and led to the kitchen, and probably the closest bathroom was through that door. On the other hand, the front door was right here, and wide open.

Muffin darted in the front door, going for the bathroom with the homing instinct of a migrating bird.

How Cinda would treasure these photographs in the years to come!

Kit got out of her Volvo and circled it, and as she turned she counted three cars parked in the space between the house and the garage. One was Ed's scary, long low Caddy. The other two were Jeep Grand Cherokees, high and square, one red, one navy blue. They were facing out, ready to leave, like Kit, and they were filled. Packed. Jammed with boxes and bags and stuff.

Don't be silly, she said to herself. The cars aren't facing out. Cinda and Burt are moving in, at this very moment.

Kit took a shot of the row of cars, to immortalize moving day, and a shot of the house, to immortalize the flowers in bloom on the day the baby came. The flower photo might not come out, because there was so little light, but the cars would be clear. They didn't have Jersey plates. In fact, she noticed, each Jeep had the plate of a different state. Perhaps Cinda and Burt had just gotten married! Perhaps they were merging households for the very first time, and — no, that didn't make sense. People struggling to adopt had always been married for ages.

Cinda held the baby to her breast and tucked her head against his. "He smells so sweet."

Kit smiled to herself. That would soon be incorrect. She moved the camera to vertical position for the next picture.

Ed Bing caught her shoulder. "Hey! No photographs! I'll take the camera!" He actually had the nerve to put his fat hand on top of hers, trying to get the camera away from her! She wanted to kick him in the shins. Kit wrenched away from him, glaring.

"Photographs!" said Burt. The man Kit assumed was Burt.

"Of course you want photographs," said Kit. "This is such an important day! The first day you ever had your son. Now you'll have pictures to cherish forever."

The laughter left Cinda's face. The cigarette was lowered from Ed's mouth. The watch no longer interested Burt. They stared at Kit. She stared back.

"I'm so sorry we're so jumpy, Kit," said

Cinda. "It's just been a very difficult day for us all."

"For me, too," said Kit. She thought, They're too nervous to introduce themselves. They haven't even said the baby's name. They must have chosen a name. They've known about him for days. "Are you Burt Chance?" she said to the second man.

He snapped, a severe head-to-toe muscle spasm, as if he'd had an electric jolt. "How does she know our name?" Burt said roughly to Cinda.

"I told her on the phone, when I was asking her to bring the baby," said Cinda, in an oddly pleading voice.

Burt seemed furious and badly upset, almost weepy, and now for the second time he touched Sam the Baby's cheek, and ran a finger gently across the downy hair on Sam's head.

Ed moved forward in a strange, herding sort of way, like a dog moving sheep to slaughter. His mouth was open too much and he was breathing heavily and his eyes were too wide, rotating from Cinda to Kit to Burt to Cinda — but never to the baby. His cousin's little boy.

The day ended. Dusk thickened into night. Kit could not hear them breathing.

She could barely see their faces. She could not see Muffin at all.

Kit pressed the button for the flash, in order to take the precious picture of the three of them: mother, father, and son for the first moment in their lives. She looked down to check the signal light. When it came on, she lifted the camera and saw that the three grown-ups were paying no attention to the baby. Their focus was on Kit. The baby had slid off Cinda's shoulder and was halfway down her arm, and Cinda had not noticed.

Kit's arms chilled beneath her sleeves. Her hair prickled. She remembered the day when Mom had sat her down to announce that there would be a separation and then a divorce, because Mom had found "somebody else." Mom's expressions had been fake and out of place. Her smiles had come at the wrong times. Her excitement had been a complete mismatch for the occasion.

And this — this moment — these people — they were a complete mismatch for the occasion.

Why hadn't Cinda rushed inside to get the cute little clothing she must have bought for this long-awaited moment? How could she let her new son go on wearing nothing but his blanket and his Huggies?

Why was Ed standing there, panting like a hound?

Why was Burt so upset? Why was he looking at his watch instead of his son?

I should have called Dad, thought Kit. So what if he doesn't like being bothered? So what if Dusty is a pain? *This is a baby.* I've treated Sam like part of Dusty's doll collection.

Collection.

It was a collection of people, but one of them was missing.

Where is Muffin? she thought.

"How sweet of you, Kit." Cinda's voice was getting higher with each sentence. It was trembling now, too. "How thoughtful to be thinking of our baby book. I have a grand idea! Ed, let's get Kit in a photograph. After all, she brought us our baby. Kit, give Ed the camera. We need you in the picture." Cinda handed Sam the Baby to Kit.

The baby was warm and limp in her arms. Spineless. There was something eerie about his bonelessness, as if Kit had all the bones and he had none. She tucked Sam into her own body, but it was not successful; she could not wrap around him; she could not hide him. First Dusty left Sam as easily as she would have left a package. Now Cinda had handed him off as if he didn't matter.

"Why didn't you pick up the baby at the hospital?" asked Kit.

The house had no furniture in it.

There was not a chair. Not a couch. Not a TV. Not a table.

Muffin walked through a hall with stairs going up, but she didn't go up them, and instead went into what had to be the living room — and nobody lived there.

Boxes and papers littered the floor. Crumpled computer printouts carpeted the room. Brown paper grocery bags overflowed with more crumpled paper.

Muffin found the powder room off the kitchen and there was one towel in there and a roll of toilet paper sitting on the floor. There was no soap. Still, it was a bathroom, and Muffin was very glad to sit on the toilet for a minute. Then she went into the kitchen to find soap. Her mother believed in frequent hand washing.

If you used nothing else in your whole house, you had to use your kitchen. Everybody loved food, even health people like Mom, who outlawed so many types of food.

There were stacks of empty greasy pizza boxes, from many different places, as if these grown-ups had decided to try every pizza place in New Jersey, and never the same one twice.

Muffin opened the drawer next to the sink. It did not hold silver and it did not hold knives. It was empty. She opened two cabinets. They were empty.

The kitchen was dirty.

Aunt Karen's house was not clean and it was not neat. But it had a comfortable feel to it. This kitchen had an awful filth grime to it.

Muffin was afraid.

New babies — didn't they get sick easily? Shouldn't their mommies be very concerned with health?

One of these people smoked, they didn't have soap in the bathroom, they didn't even own dishes?

Muffin agonized over being nine. If she were sixteen, like Rowen, or thirty-eight, like Dad, she would know things.

She knew only that she did not want Sam the Baby here.

She did not want to drive away and know that her clean sweet baby was in the hands of people who did not even keep a chair to sit on.

She remembered when the people across the street had their first baby. They shopped for nine months. They had clothes and toys and a bassinet and a carriage and music boxes and books for parental guidance and new wallpaper.

Sam the Baby had used his last Huggie and his last baby wipe and he had only one of the little disposable bottles left.

Now what?

Who were these people who lived way out here without soap and weren't ready for their own baby to arrive?

Chapter 7

Muffin came out of the house.

Lights were on inside, so Muffin was framed in the doorway. Backlit, she looked exceptionally small: a kindergarten drawing; a stick figure. Kit knew that little sisters were pretty tough, but Muffin didn't look tough. She looked as if she could be snapped along any bone.

"Hey!" said Burt roughly, spotting Muffin. "Hey! What were you doing inside our house?" He whirled, slamming his feet down, heading for the door. He was not a big man, he was not as tall as Kit, but suddenly his entire body was a threat: was muscle: was force.

If I need to protect Muffin, I can't do it, thought Kit. My arms are full of baby.

She remembered a game that had been popular at slumber parties in California.

You drew a card with some dreadful moral question. "If the house is on fire, and there are three children in the house, ages one and four and seven, and you can save only one — which one do you save?"

It's a real question, thought Kit, and fear creased her mind like a fold on a final exam: *I can save only one.*

Cinda caught Burt's sleeve, whispering, "I was the one who called them, Burt! Don't be mad at the little girl. I had to call! It was our last chance to get Dusty's baby!"

How frantic the whisper was! How pierced with anxiety!

Burt shook her off, but he did stop moving.

Muffin came down the first step. Cinda, Ed, and Burt did not take their eyes off her, as if she were a carrier of a disease and they must watch where she went. What is going on here? thought Kit. How can they be afraid of Muffin?

Kit knew Muffin and Rowen's mother slightly. Mrs. Mason never said, "You are to be back here at precisely nine o'clock, and not a minute later," which was the kind of order Kit received. Muffin's mother said things like, "Trust your instincts.

What does your body tell you? What is the aura?"

The aura rots, thought Kit.

"I had to use your bathroom," said Muffin with dignity. "You don't have any soap. Don't you wash your hands afterwards? Now that you have Sam, you need to remember to wash your hands frequently."

Her voice was frail in the dark and the silence of this remote place. It was a strange stranded copy of her own mother's voice.

Sam isn't the baby's name, thought Kit. I made it up. How come Cinda and Burt aren't correcting her? How come they're not saying, "Oh, no, this is Conor! Spencer! Dennis! Shane!" or whatever name they have ready?

"Are you moving out or are you moving in?" said Muffin.

"We're not settled yet, are we?" agreed Cinda. She was holding her husband's arm, as if they were about to go down an aisle together. "We're such a mess. You must forgive us. Now, what is your name, honey? Tell us your name."

"My name is Muffin. I'm Sam's babysitter. I looked at every one of your boxes. You don't have any Huggies. You're going to need lots of them," she said, a teacher now, shaking her voice like a finger at people who just won't learn.

"Listen, kid . . ." said Ed, in a voice so harsh it scraped every nerve in Kit's body.

She had to draw their attention away from Muffin. In her calmest voice, as if she were a school secretary who had seen everything, seen through every lie, been bored by every problem, she said, "I'd like to see the paperwork for this adoption. What did Dusty sign?"

If she needed to get out of here, she had faith in her body. She could outrun these people, maneuver more quickly, leap and parry and get away, on foot or in her car. But she had two children with her. She felt like a mother fox carrying kits in her mouth, trying desperately to move them one by one to safety — but she had to abandon the rest each time she saved the one.

Her ploy worked. They swerved in a chorus line to face her.

"Now, Kit," said Ed Bing, "this is in the family." He had managed to remove some of the harshness in his voice, but it lay beneath, like a bear trap under old leaves. His hands were out, his ten puffy yellow fingers stretching, but she could not tell exactly what he was reaching for. She held the baby tighter.

"We don't have any social workers or anything like that involved," he said. "Dusty lived with Cinda and Burt for a while, and even worked for them, and the four of us are very close." While he was talking, Ed passed Kit's camera to Burt, who clicked his key ring, and one of the Jeeps made an answering beep, and its interior lights came on. The car was full in a messy, tipping, tilting, desperate sort of way. Boxes and stuff had been thrown in.

Kit had moved. When you moved, you had to pack the car with extraordinary care: every box neatly on top of the other, filling every inch, so that nothing shifted or fell or was at risk. Because the moving van had most of your stuff: In your car, you put only the really necessary and really precious things.

Burt crossed the grass — black, and not green, in the darkening night — to his Jeep, and when he opened the back door, he had to catch stuff tumbling out. He set the camera — Kit's camera; her property! — on top of the piles of junk in his car.

"We have to leave now," said Burt from his side of the yard. He was talking to Cinda. "We have to leave *now*."

So the Grand Cherokees *were* facing out. They were ready for — for what? The word that came to Kit's mind was *flight*.

And Ed's long low scary hulk of a car — was it parked to block them?

"Burt, I can't bear to leave our baby behind! I love him already," whispered Cinda, turning back to Sam. But she did not attempt to take him from Kit. She stared at him, as if he were completely and always somebody else's child; as if she had no rights.

Leave the baby behind?

"No!" shouted Ed. His voice slammed like a door. "No! Cinda, that baby is yours! We are staying with the plan." He was bellowing. There was no need; it was very quiet in this remote clearing; he could have stage-whispered and they would all have heard just fine.

They were spread over the dark yard: Muffin near the house, Kit and Sam by the car, Cinda hovering, Ed panting like a hound at her back, Burt on the far side of the gravel drive, next to his car, rattling his keys.

"I didn't think things would work out like this," said Burt. He was whiny, like a toddler who needed a nap. Then, as abruptly as that toddler, his voice switched to anger. “You should never have called them!” he yelled at Cinda. “I can’t believe you called them!”

He’s going to have a temper tantrum, thought Kit.

Muffin came up behind Kit. She not only pressed up against Kit’s thigh, but actually latched her fingers through the belt loops of Kit’s pants. Kit was hugely relieved to have her tiny family — her one-hour-old family — pressed up against her. Sam in her arms, Muffin at her side.

Ed came closer to Kit, and now the puffed ugly fingers, all ten of them, seemed to reach for Sam.

In her little flute voice Muffin said, “They don’t even have chairs, Kit. And there isn’t any furniture in those cars. They’ve been here, but they haven’t eaten anything in weeks but pizza. Plus they didn’t throw away their pizza boxes. They’re going to get bugs.”

“May I hold Sam?” said Cinda. Cinda was crying.

Kit was not letting go of Sam. She backed up against her unlocked car. Shifting Sam against her chest, gripping him crosswise with one arm and hand, she managed to reach behind herself and get the back door open. She schooled her voice:

It must remain calm. The only way to do this was with her Dullness Training. Calm was the one thing that actually startled people. They did not know what to do about confidence, except stand there and watch you be confident. "Get in the car, Muffin," she said easily.

Muffin scrambled in.

Cinda and Burt were still yelling across the grass. Ed seemed ready to fly at Cinda, seemed ready to strangle her!

Kit dreaded having to put Sam into his carrier. It was not a quick procedure, and she would have her back to all of them. And then she still had to walk all the way around the car. Do it now, do it efficiently, she told herself. She leaned in and over Muffin to pop Sam into his seat. Muffin had the straps up and nodded to let Kit know that she would finish the job. Sam's little body flung itself outward when Kit shifted him, and he whimpered, his little fists curling and uncurling. How scary to live in a world that could do what it wanted with your body.

"Tell you what," said Kit, shutting the door on Muffin, "come to Dad's house in the morning, Cinda. Dusty will be there by then, and we'll sort this out." She clicked her key ring, locking all four doors. "It just feels a little messy to me," she said casually. There. Muffin and Sam were okay. They were in the fortress of the Volvo. Even if Ed or Burt or Cinda got the key ring away from her and clicked it, Muffin could override the command and keep the car locked. Muffin was no fool. She was already reaching in between the two front seats to find the driver's control.

Cinda began to cry, flinging looks at her husband, at Ed, at Kit, at the baby.

"No!" said Ed. "No! You promised! We're doing this!"

"Give it up, Ed," said Burt. His voice sagged. "We're out of time. It didn't work. You're not getting all your money."

Money? thought Kit. She was walking carefully around the car, hoping Ed would not try to intercept her. She knew Burt wouldn't. She didn't think Cinda would.

But Ed . . .

He was that thing you heard references to in TV games . . . a wild card.

And also, a wild car. Once he got behind the wheel of that Caddy, both driver and vehicle would be wild. And it was the first car in line, facing out. If they followed Kit, it would be Ed at the front of the line.

Money, she thought. There's money sometimes in private adoptions. Is Ed being paid by Cinda and Burt? If Sam the Baby isn't delivered, Ed doesn't get the rest of his money? And Dusty? What did she get paid? Is this about money, then? Not about my precious little guy's life and future and the people who love him?

But money?

Kit hated Dusty then.

It was a sharp clean emotion, which she would not have expected, because she had certainly never hated her mother for anything, no matter how upset she'd been over the years, and she never hated Malcolm, only disliked him for existing. She would have thought hate would be a big splat of shuddering dislike.

But it was blade thin, slicing Dusty like peel from an orange.

A brand-new life, a trusting sleeping perfect baby, and Dusty just threw everything into the mixing bowl and let it get whipped up.

Muffin leaned between the seats and opened the driver's door for Kit.

"No," said Cinda, weeping openly. "No, please, you don't understand. I've wanted a baby for so long! And this was perfect! Everything was perfectly planned, and I will be a good mother, I will! Kit, we can't come in the morning. You see, we have other problems. We have financial problems and —"

"Stop talking about it!" shouted Burt.

"She has to understand!" sobbed Cinda. "I need that baby. He's mine. We all agreed on that. Dusty didn't want a baby! She didn't want a baby at all, even for a minute!"

Then why weren't you at the hospital? thought Kit. She got into the car, trying not to lose her Dullness Training skills, trying not to tremble, or vomit, or scream, or catch her own fingers in the door from slamming it so fast.

"No!" said Ed. He launched himself at the car, tearing at the back door handle, which he knew, they all knew, was locked solidly. "You leave that baby here!"

Kit thrust the key into the ignition.

Ed was pawing at the windows now, and Muffin shrank back, her hands spread out in front of Sam, to protect him from the evil of Ed's eyes.

"No, Ed!" cried Cinda. "No, no, no, you calm down. We all have to calm down here. Let's calm down." She took Ed's arm and led him away from the car.

"I want my money!" shouted Ed Bing. He pulled clear of Cinda, put his two palms flat on the hood, and she thought of his half-moon palm edges on the glass doors. Now his fingerprints were on her car; if something really really terrible happened, the police would find those fingerprints.

Kit started the engine.

"Kit, you're getting us all upset over nothing," said Ed Bing. The hum of the motor made it difficult to hear him. "Roll your window down," he yelled. "We're all very emotional because this is such a tiny baby, and Dusty has not been rational, you know how difficult Dusty is — your father left her because of that! — and you know that she is not a good person to bring up a baby — and Cinda and Burt have wanted a baby for years, and they will make the best parents of all."

"They didn't even buy Huggies!" Muffin shouted back. "They don't have soap in their bathroom. I bet they don't own a crib." Muffin lowered her voice. "Just drive away, Kit. We'll go to Shea's house and my Aunt Karen will know what to do."

Ed Bing was leaning over the hood now, pocked face distorted with yelling, like some huge insect caught on her windshield.

"Drive over him," said Muffin. "He'll look better squashed."

"We're out of time!" shouted Burt.

Cinda was hanging on to Ed and losing her balance, so that she, too, was half leaning on the Volvo. Cinda called, "Really, I understand, Kit. I'm glad you're thinking of the baby first. Please just forget about all this. Dusty — Dusty will — Dusty —"

But Cinda had no idea what Dusty would do; nobody knew what Dusty would do; probably least of all, Dusty.

"Kit! What do we have to do, call the police?" yelled Ed Bing. "You are kidnapping Cinda and Burt's child!"

Burt came loping across the grass at last, and for a minute Kit thought he was going to land on the roof of the Volvo, and she would have all three of them clinging to her car, and —

But he was offering money to Ed. Ed stepped toward Burt's wallet.

Burt said, "Kit, just take the kid and leave. It didn't work. We're very sorry you got involved in this. It wasn't my idea, okay? Please just forget all about it. Come on, Cinda, we gotta get out of here. Now!"

Kit put the car in drive. "Wave to them, Muffin," she whispered. "Make this look normal." Kit pressed the accelerator.

They were ten feet away. Twenty feet. Thirty.

And then a hundred feet, two hundred,

almost out of the driveway, almost safe in the woods that had seemed so unsafe before.

Muffin Mason opened her window. She stuck her head all the way out, her shoulders at risk from tree branches. She yelled in her sturdiest voice, "Anyway, there were *two* cameras! I took plenty of pictures, too! So we still have pictures of Sam the Baby even if you stole Kit's camera. So there!"

CHAPTER 8

Rowen calculated that half the cars in New Jersey drove around just to drive around. Nobody had a destination. Everybody was cruising, listening to the radio, not thinking of much. To keep his mind busy, Row was trying to figure out how that ATM scam had worked. It was complex. According to the radio reports, the criminals had manufactured a couple of ATM machines of their own and put them illegally in public places like malls. People went up and stuck their bank cards in to get cash and the machines copied down their account number and PIN number, which the criminals now had. Then the bad guys made their own bank cards, and using the PIN number — supposedly known only to the card carrier — they could hit any real ATM machine anywhere in the country and get money out of the victims' bank accounts.

It was clever, and yet, Row didn't see how it could really work.

You'd have a bushel basket of fake bank cards, and in order to use them, you'd have to carry around your printout with the PIN numbers. Then what did you do? Line up with regular customers at an ATM, getting your money a hundred or two hundred dollars at a time? Did you run ten cards through the machine while other people waited behind you? And how many ATMs did you go to? Because the bank machines were programmed not to allow too many withdrawals at a time — it was suspicious.

So did you just cruise the state — or several states, because according to the radio, the scam was up and going in Pennsylvania and New York and Connecticut as well — looking for ATM machines?

Row himself cruised down a street he had driven about ten times already in the last hour, because he was circling near Kit's two houses and near Shea's, so that he could intercept them.

He was too worried and too disgusted with himself to show up at Shea's and wait. He could imagine so well, so painfully well, what his aunt and uncle and cousin would say to him.

He put his mind on crime once more.

In your fake ATM, which you were using just to get the bank card numbers to start with, no money would be distributed to customers. Some customers would just grit their teeth and forget it, but wouldn't the rest call in the ATM failure? And wouldn't the bank realize they didn't *have* an ATM at that location? And wouldn't that bring the police? So didn't that mean that you'd be constantly picking up and moving your fake ATM to fake locations? And wouldn't that increase your risk something fierce?

Row had a fantasy in which he himself was a master criminal. Not the scummy type that ripped off innocent old ladies' retirement money in investment plans that didn't exist — but some cool fabulous way of stealing cool fabulous things — like diamonds from mines. He was a little concerned by his fantasy, since his father was the type just to shoot him if he even expressed it, but he liked his fantasy, and pulled it out fairly often; he could really get into his plans for the Big, Big Crime.

How would *he* have done the fake ATM scam, if he'd been in charge?

It seemed to him that yet another problem was that you'd have to have a crew. You'd have to have a truck to move the ATM, you'd have to have people cruising around banks to use the fake bank cards, so you could not do this alone. And the more people you had in on your scheme, the tougher it would get to keep it secret.

He remembered traffic, and took a quick glance around to be sure he wasn't driving sideways — and there, next to him, in a four-door black sedan which seemed far too tame and lacking in style, was Dusty. The ex-stepmother herself.

Such a beautiful woman! Her hair glistened tawny gold. Her earrings shimmered. She was studying herself in her own rearview mirror, and she was pleased with what she saw, tilting her head to the right and then to the left, admiring her own profile.

Rowen waved to get her attention, but she did not see him. She was pretty busy attending to herself.

When the lights changed, she drove jerkily, accelerating in little bursts and slowing in little jabs. She changed lanes without looking to see if there was space.

There was not.

Horns blared, fingers were lifted, drivers shouted unpleasant words, the syllables hidden by their closed windows. She did not notice. It was her perception that this was her own road, and she had no sense that she must share it. After several blocks, Row managed to slide in behind her. This was a woman you could follow for days and she would never know, because she was thinking only of her destination, whatever that was, and did not once glance around to see what traffic was doing.

It was astonishing such a driver was still alive.

Eventually, they arrived at Kit's father's house, which he should have guessed. She was returning for her baby. Dusty parked, walked up to the front door, and let herself in, while Row drove up right behind her. Then he reparked, because she was not likely to notice there was a car behind her and would just back into him if she left first. He pulled way to the side, using the last inch of asphalt, so she couldn't open her doors up against his car, either. She'd left the front door wide open so Rowen also just walked right into the house.

He was in time to see her beautiful ankles vanishing at the top of the stairs. "Kit!

Kit! Kit!" Dusty cried. He could hear her running from room to room, slamming many doors, as if checking closets. "Kit!" she called. "Kit, where are you?"

He waited while she rushed around the house the way she had driven around the town, and then she came racing back down the stairs.

She shrieked when she saw Rowen, so he said quickly, "I'm a friend of Kit's, Mrs. Innes. I'm Rowen Mason, we met at the club, remember you were playing tennis and my parents had friends there for dinner?" She had seemed so glamorous to Rowen — slender and gold. "The baby is fine, I saw him this afternoon, Kit's taking great care of him." As soon as the sentence was out of his mouth, he realized that Dusty had not been looking for the baby; she'd been looking for Kit.

"Oh, Rowen, of course I remember you," she said. She smiled sweetly. "You were wearing the cutest little outfit."

"The cutest little outfit?" That made him sound like Muffin. He said weakly, "Yeah, that was me."

"So the baby is fine, then," said Dusty happily. "I knew I could count on Kit. Let's get a Coke. It's the only thing you can be sure of in this house. Gavin never runs out of Coke." She set off for the kitchen. Over her shoulder, she said, "Did Kit take the baby to her mother's? That would be fine, except then I have to deal with her mother. I like Gavin's first wife; she was nice to me. But the thing is, she's sticky about things, do you know what I mean, Rowen?"

Things like — babies?

Things like — who is the father?

"I know what you mean," agreed Rowen, whose mother and father were stickier than anybody. "But Kit didn't go over to her mother's."

"Oh, I'm so glad. I just cannot get into explanations. I mean, so many people are going to be mad at me if I have to bring them into this, and I don't want to." She took a six-pack of Coke from the otherwise empty refrigerator and yanked two cans free from the plastic collar.

Rowen took his. He said, "Where were you? I mean, this afternoon. You've been gone for hours. Where did you go?"

She beamed at him. She put her long slender hand with its beautiful long slim nails up against the golden pouf of her hair and said, "I had my hair done. I just could not stand looking crummy one more minute. If anybody had told me what having a baby does to your figure and your hair, and what you have to go through after the baby is born, it's so ghastly, Rowen, and I just needed time to myself." Dusty sat gracefully on a high stool at a glossy counter and admired her hand around the Coke can. "It was so wonderful that Kit was here. It was meant. Don't you think that things are meant? That forces beyond our understanding are there with us? Helping and guiding?"

The only force behind Dusty Innes was a low IQ.

Rowen was very glad that somebody was adopting Sam the Baby. He could not begin to imagine the life an infant would have with a mother as casual as this. A mother who walked away from her newborn and figured it was "meant." He hoped Cinda was a wonderful woman, and that when Kit and Muffin came back, they'd report a happy home, and Dusty would just say, "Oh, how nice. That does give me time for myself."

Row said, "No, actually, Kit took the baby to the new parents. Cinda and Burt."

Dusty stared at him. Her smile dragged down and vanished, and she looked older. "No," she whispered. "No! I told Kit to take care of him!"

"You didn't tell Kit a single thing. You just drove away."

"It isn't my fault!" she said sharply, and suddenly Rowen could have bashed her in the face with the six-pack, and he had to step away from her, and fold his arms, and even walk back to the front hall. The glittering chandelier hanging from the second floor tossed his shadow over the black and white diamond tiles. He felt that Dusty Innes had no more substance than that shadow. But Sam — Sam the Baby — was all substance. Flesh and blood and vocal cords and staring eyes and waving toes.

"Don't be mad," she said.

As if Rowen had some power in this situation. As if Rowen mattered. "What's going on, anyway?" he demanded. "Whose baby is this?"

Dusty Innes began to cry.

"It isn't the baby that's the problem," she said. "It's the money. It just didn't work, that's all, and they promised money, and I only got half, and I wouldn't stand for it. I said, I'm getting all or nothing. So I ended up hiding out in that stupid motel waiting for them to get their money, but they don't have it! They can't have the baby. I won't be cheated out of my other half."

Rowen Mason understood very little of what Dusty was saying to him.

But one thing was clear.

She didn't care about Sam. She cared about dollars.

Kit accelerated onto the gravel drive. Even with her brights on, she felt trapped; she could see several car lengths ahead, but she had little sense of the road. She could half remember the layout she'd come in on, but it was completely different going this direction; she could not get her bearings. Gravel spurted like BB shots. "What did you do that for?" she screamed at Muffin. "What did you tell them about your camera for?"

"They thought they were so great," said Muffin, "and I wanted them to know they aren't!" Muffin had loved leaning out the window. Loved her moment of bragging. It had been like yelling, *So there!* at a bully on the playground. But the trouble with bullies was, they were bigger. And in this case, the bullies had three cars. "I'm sorry," whispered Muffin.

Behind them, way back, poked the double lights of a following car.

Who was coming after them? Or were they all coming, and she could glimpse only the first? She had no money. She could not supply Ed with his payment.

Sam the Baby had begun to cry. It was big lusty crying, as if he'd gained ten pounds, all in the lungs. The crying scraped Kit's brain, and Muffin kept saying, "What's wrong, Sam? What's wrong? Kit, I don't know what's wrong."

"As soon as we get on pavement, he'll be fine. He doesn't like being bounced like this." They're not coming after Muffin and me, thought Kit. They're not coming after Sam, either. They're coming for the camera. Suddenly she knew that.

"Where's the camera, Muff?" she said. "We might just throw it at them, if they catch up to us."

"Like throwing a steak to an attack dog," agreed Muffin.

They reached the pavement. Kit turned in the direction of home. She felt like a carrier pigeon. Released from the cage of her stupid decision, she was going home. Home was a place she could find no matter what obstacles they put in her path. Even in the dark, even on strange roads, she knew exactly which direction home was.

I have three houses, she thought. Dad's in California, Dad's in New Jersey, Mom's in New Jersey. But home is Mom's. Mom and Malcolm's. I hope they didn't go out to dinner. I hope they didn't go to a movie. I hope they're home.

Not a single blank page of her Dullness Training existed within her right now. She was shaking and furious and afraid. The only thing that seemed to work well was her right foot, which slammed to the floor. She turned off Swamp Maple and onto Hennicot. I didn't see any cars on the way here, she said to herself, so I'm not going to see cars on the way back.

She whipped down Hennicot.

Muffin said, "You're going too fast."

Kit struggled for the calm she had mastered. Where had it gone? Now when she needed it, how could it have left? She was a whole other person: she was a collection of ragged nerves, shaking hands, and one lead foot. I've got to think, she thought. I've got to think.

But the only thought that came to mind was getting home.

After the second scream of tires, she knew Muffin was right. A car accident was more likely right now than dealing with Ed and Cinda and Burt. This being a grown-up stuff was complex. You had to save the baby and also not crash the car.

What was on the camera that scared

them? What had they been doing in their empty house that was more important than the arrival of their new baby? Why was Burt so urgent about leaving right now — why had Cinda known that they could not take the baby after all?

The baby was crying harder. His crying was raw, desperate, as if terrible pain assailed him.

"Feed him," said Kit. "Give him that last bottle."

But Sam would not put his mouth around the nipple.

"Cuddle him," said Kit. "Rub his tummy. Kiss his cheek."

Sam just yelled louder.

"I hate him now," said Muffin. "I'm doing all I can and he isn't paying attention."

Kit knew nothing about babies. What if he was having appendicitis? What if his little insides had knotted up and split and gotten infected? What if she had given him old tired milk spouting with bacteria and viruses and dread disease?

Swamp Maple and Hennicot Road and Dexter Mill were much shorter going home than they had been going away. Was that literally true? Had she been crawling along before, trying to find the next turn? So that every mile seemed like ten?

Her mind spun. She felt like a kindergartner who had whirled in circles over the entire playground, until her brain had lost its hold.

She had forgotten about being followed.

How weird; how weird the loss of her calm was!

Get home, she said to herself very firmly. Just concentrate on getting home.

She had to slow down quite a bit for the entrance to Route 80. There were red lights, and turn lanes to get in, and she had enough brain to remember that she wanted 80 East, because that led home.

Muffin said, "Kit! They caught up to us," and Kit froze. Now even her eyes did not work. They flared open and stuck there, as if they were pinned, and she could not use them anymore; she needed to blink to get focus, and blinks did not come.

A horn behind them began tapping. Not a furious get-out-of-my-face type honk, which was a New Jersey specialty — but a sort of friendly, hi, how are you? kind of honk.

Kit sat in the intersection without a thought in her brain.

It felt as if Sam the Baby's screams were coming out of her own chest. She could no more think than Sam could: Infants had no vocabulary for thoughts; Sam could only yell; and *she* had no vocabulary for thoughts; Kit could only struggle to use whatever Muffin had to say.

"It's Burt," said Muffin. "Kit! Drive! He's getting out of his car! He's coming toward us! He's walking on the road, right here in the middle of traffic!"

Kit managed to find her rearview mirror on the outside of her door. She managed to see a person in it. She read, *Objects in the mirror are closer than they appear.* This did not comfort her.

The light stayed red. Many directions of traffic had to take turns. It wasn't Kit's turn.

Burt was striding forward, his hand was extended, and she knew that he wanted the door handle, and even though all four doors were locked and it would take crowbars to get into a locked Volvo, the thought of his fingers closing on her personal door was horrifying.

We're out of time, Burt had said. He had meant real time: wristwatch time. He and Cinda, but apparently not Ed, were facing some deadline. Something that required them to pack by hurling their possessions into their cars, not sorting, not stacking. Their cars had been facing out. Ready for what?

Ready to go somewhere without a baby.

Because the cars had not had space for a passenger.

Kit gave up trying to think clearly. She couldn't even think muddy. Kit drove through the red.

There was opposing traffic. A huge double truck, jointed in the middle, was approaching the ramp where Kit had to drive. Behind it, two cars and a van were lined up. Kit prayed for room, passed all four of them on the right — the worst and stupidest thing in driving — because the other drivers did not expect you and would flatten you. But the ramp was slightly uphill, the truck had gathered no speed, and she made it. She got ahead of the double truck, and Burt did not even get on the ramp.

"Wow," said Muffin. "Do they give you medals for that, or arrest you?"

Kit flew down the road. Route 80 had enough traffic to stock the East Coast. She did not risk a glance at her speedometer. She didn't want to know. She felt like a heroine and like a total jerk. She felt clever and supremely, hideously stupid.

What is happening? she thought. Are these bad guys? Are they really Burt and Cinda Chance? Did they make up being cousins? I bet they made up the name Chance. Nobody's last name is Chance.

Were these people taking some great Chance? Were they involved in some huge gamble? Was the Chance a chance to get a baby? But if that was the Chance they were after, why would Burt have ignored the baby? So it was some other Chance.

We're out of time.

A huge rectangular sign with sparkling night-light letters proclaimed an exit in half a mile. Now Kit realized that the edge of the road was peppered with signs. She had been way too busy not getting into a crash to do any reading. At this exit would be restaurants, gas, diesel fuel, telephones, motels — the works. Kit whipped herself into the slow lane, turned down the exit, and got off 80.

"What are you doing?" cried Muffin. "We aren't home! This isn't home! We can't get off here! We don't even know where this is!"

Kit turned right and merged into light traffic. There were fast-food places, superstores, convenience stores, and lights. Many, many lights. Her plain old navy blue

Volvo looked like one leaf in a leaf pile. She pulled into the parking lot of a twenty-four-hour store and backed into a slot. If Burt showed up, she'd know.

But her bet was that Burt would still be flying down 80.

He would not try to find her on 80. He would assume she was going to her father's house. He would try to intercept her there. Probably Burt had a car phone. Ed knew about Dad's house, so if Ed wasn't driving right along in Burt's path, which he probably was, Ed would tell Burt how to get to Dad's house.

But Dad's was difficult to find. In the dark, only luck would bring Burt to the right golf course entrance, the right circular road, the right dead end, and the right house. Kit doubted if Burt could locate it.

Then she thought, No. Burt will give up. He's out of time. Whatever's on the camera, he'll just have to shrug about. They can't take the baby, somehow both he and Cinda knew that. Even Ed knew that, but he was pretending to himself that they would take Sam and he would get paid.

What could be on that camera film?

She herself had photographed the people, the flowers, the cars —

Cars.

She had gotten their license plates.

Two different states. The numbers and letters, which Kit could not remember, had been clear when she focused the camera.

Who cared if somebody knew their license plate number?

Enough time had passed. None of her possible pursuers had gotten off Route 80. They were safe here. Kit went into the convenience store and bought a new pack of diapers. Then she got bagels and cream cheese for Muffin and herself. It turned out that she was too nervous to eat, but Muffin wasn't.

There was a telephone for drivers to use out their windows, so she pulled up to it and called Mom. No answer.

Kit had known there would be no answer. Mom and Malcolm loved movies. With Kit safely spending the night at Shea's, heavily chaperoned by a dozen pets and the always vigilant Aunt Karen, Mom and Malcolm could go to two movies, back to back, and they would not think about Kit for a minute.

She called Dad in California. No answer. There was a three-hour time difference, though. He'd be at work. She called his office. They said he was in Seattle. She said what hotel? They said he wouldn't have checked in yet.

Muffin said, "Let's go to Aunt Karen's. She'll know if Sam the Baby is just cranky or if we should go to the hospital."

Sam's crying had not diminished. He was an athlete for crying. He was Olympian; he had only a few pounds of himself, and they were all rage and sobs and heaves.

"Or maybe the police," said Kit. She couldn't think through the mud of the situation. It seemed amazing that she could be an honor roll student. Was she doing it without a brain?

Now she was immobilized, as if the best choice were just to sit here in the parking lot and not eat her bagel, while Sam screamed and traffic went by.

Muffin nodded. "Let's call 911. On TV they're always nice to you even if you are stupid. So even if Burt and Cinda *are* adopting, and *we're* the kidnappers, 911 people will be nice to us. Yes. Call the 911 people. People in uniforms have sirens and their lights will twirl around."

It was comforting to think of official lights twirling around. Of adults who possessed thinking abilities, and probably had rescued enough people that they didn't have to do Dullness Training; it was dull to them; they would just say, Oh, another newborn whose mother sold him and another teenager who drove off into the night without a thought.

Without a thought.

She was truly in that position. She was without a thought.

"You're right, Muff. I'm just going to make one more call before we hit 911."

Kit called Dad's house in Seven Hills, hoping desperately that Dusty would pick up the phone, because Dusty's errands were over by now and Dusty would tell Kit what was going on and what to do, although Dusty was not known for being able to tell other people what to do — and Rowen answered the phone.

CHAPTER 9

In fifteen minutes, they were back at Dad's house, which was lit from every downstairs window, with the outside spotlights on, and a little row of ground lights illuminating the sidewalk like an airport runway. Muffin leaped out of the car as her brother flung open the front door, and Kit, in perfect imitation of Dusty hours earlier, struggled with the straps to scoop up the baby.

Sam was still yelling. His tiny chest heaved with effort, his lungs punishing big people the only way he knew.

Kit came in the big foyer, amazed by how much light there was: light from the enormous chandelier hanging from the second floor; light reflected from the gleaming black and white tiles; light bouncing off mirrors. The baby squinted, and she cradled him in the shade of her hand.

Dusty was upon her like an attack dog. "How could you do that, Kit? How could you go someplace? I trusted you! I counted on you to stay here! Cinda and Burt! I can't believe you did that!"

Immediately things were normal. She had a thought. She had a ton of thoughts. "You're the who can't be counted on! You threw Sam into this house without a single explanation! He could have been a UPS package! A box with a bar code! You didn't tell me one single thing. You didn't even tell me his name." Kit remembered now that she hated Dusty. And looking at this woman who had dumped her son, she thought, Dusty's beautiful again! She's had her hair done! Did she leave her baby so she could go to the salon? I don't believe it.

"Why is he screaming like that?" demanded Dusty. "What have you been doing?"

"I don't know why he's screaming like that. He's *your* baby. *You* comfort him." Kit felt like shoving Dusty through the window glass or into the microwave. She closed her arms around Sam, sorry she had suggested that Dusty even touch Sam, let alone attempt to comfort him. She had not given Sam up to Cinda, or to Ed, and she was not giving him up to Dusty, either.

Her head suddenly ached. She felt physically terrible. Conked over and over again with a stone, maybe, right behind her eyes. Poor Sam the Baby. Did he feel this terrible?

Dusty quit having hysterics. The tantrum had been faked. Kit could remember whole rows of tantrums, back during the divorce. Dad simply got on a plane and found sanctuary on another coast. Kit remembered herself defending Dusty; being friends with Dusty; sympathizing with Dusty — and now she could see that it had been Dusty's style, not Dusty's heart.

Dusty's lovely features came together in a pout, so she looked remarkably like Muffin, age nine, unwilling to touch icky diapers.

In Kit's arms, the baby was sweaty and hot, and the sobs had diminished to a scratchy level, as if he were giving himself a sore throat. He needed a bath, he needed a flat place to lie down, he needed —

Everything, thought Kit. That's what a baby is: need. Sam needs everything.

Her heart broke.

Whatever else had happened in her own family; whatever ways her mother had not measured up to what Kit had wanted; whatever ways her father and stepfather had chosen to behave — they were minor. She had been adored from birth, and nobody had ever abandoned her, or ever would.

Kit brushed past Dusty and went into the family room, where the big green leather couch still looked like a couch on the department store floor, and where nothing in the room felt affectionate, and warm, and right for a baby.

Rowen came after her. "Here's what's happening. Dusty's cousin Ed arranged a private adoption. The couple are Cinda and Burt Chance. They're paying Dusty fifty thousand dollars to get her baby, and they gave her half of it up front. They are also paying Ed fifty thousand. She signed papers selling her kid to them. She's afraid she'll go to prison for selling her baby if anybody finds out about it."

Oh, Sam the Baby, thought Kit, and her heart and soul doubled over in pain for him. He *was* a sale item. He *did* have a bar code. Dusty *had* shipped him.

Kit walked over to the kitchen sinks: shining pale yellow porcelain, with a delicate pattern of flowers rimming the edges, as if the sink were a vase. She had no idea what was in the drawers around the sink, and began flinging them open. Sure enough, the decorator had filled the drawers. She pulled out a pile of lovely, never-used tea towels.

Everybody gathered around her at the sink, crowding up to her, as if she were the mommy, with the answers, or the dinner ready to serve.

"So Dusty doesn't want police involved," Row went on.

Kit unwrapped the damp flannel baby blanket, peeled off the wet diaper, and lay Sam carefully on a bed of dish towels. In another drawer she found a little terrycloth square, held it under just-right warm water, wrung it out, and began sponging him down.

If anything, Sam hated this more. His little muscles went rigid trying to fight her off, but he did not know how to use his tiny arms and legs and she held him down easily. Muffin opened the new diaper pack and unfolded one for Kit. Even in this terrible situation, Kit was tickled by the teensiness of the diaper and the baby who would wear it.

"But," said Rowen, "Dusty does want to stop the adoption, because when she met them, she didn't like Cinda and Burt."

"Well, I'm glad to hear that!" said Muffin, and Kit realized that Muffin, like Kit herself a year ago, was on Dusty's side. What amazing abilities Dusty possessed! Dusty could charm people on to her side, even people as sophisticated and cynical as her own father. Even a little girl as sturdy and clear-eyed as Muffin Mason. "You are absolutely right, Dusty," said Muffin. "There is something wrong with those people. They don't have soap in their bathroom. They don't eat anything but pizza and they steal cameras."

"They steal cameras?" repeated Rowen, staring at his sister.

Kit flung towels around until she found a nice soft large one to wrap Sam in. It was warm in the house, but she didn't want him bare. It looked drafty. He did not stop crying, however. Drafts were apparently not his problem.

"Sam's mad at us for getting his life wrong," said Muffin. "I would be pretty mad if my mother dumped me." She looked hard at Dusty, and Kit felt better; Muffin *had* seen through this shallow woman. Kit found a smile rising to her face, the first one in hours. I love Muffin, too, she thought. I really did adopt a family this afternoon. Muffin is mine, Sam is mine.

She looked at Row to see if Rowen was hers, too, but Row was staring at his sister, with a tense frown and stiff shoulders. He was holding his breath. He gave the impression of Sam's opposite: Sam could function only if he used his breath screaming, and Row could function only if he didn't use any breath at all.

"And," said Muffin, "the people who wanted to adopt him are in a witch's coven."

"Muff," said her brother. "Nobody's in a witch's coven. They want a baby, is all. They want a baby enough to pay for it. Dusty didn't like them and tried to break it off, and everybody went off the deep end. Of course they were frantic. This is just a matter of calming down."

Dusty's eyes flickered. Her lips moved, as if to correct Row, and then she looked away and shifted a Coke can in her lovely hands.

"Let me hold him," said Row. He took Sam as if he held babies all the time. "Poor little guy," he said crooningly. "People have really thrown you around today, haven't they? You don't know anybody good, do you?"

"*I'm* good," said Muffin. "*Kit's* good."

Rowen wrapped the baby tightly in his little towel, fastening down the flailing arms and legs, and then he wrapped his own arms around Sam and rested his long heavy jaw against Sam's tiny face.

Sam snuffled.

Sam hiccuped.

Sam slept.

They rejoiced in the silence. Sam went from being a nightmare to being his beautiful little self again.

"You have a future in child care, Row," said Kit.

She saw him so clearly as a father; saw him nestling up next to his own baby boy; saw him coming home early from work to do his share, to cuddle his kid. Then she backed up from the father vision and put herself and Row in a wedding together, and then she backed up from that and gave them a first date.

All this took one second.

She found herself laughing.

"The guys had to take a course last year," explained Rowen. "It was called 'Boy, Oh, Boy — Babies!' We didn't learn a single thing about babies because no mother was willing to donate a baby for us to learn on. We were supposed to use dolls, but none of the boys would touch them."

"But you got an A, didn't you?" said Muffin, happy to see Sam snooze. Just when you decided an older brother was good for nothing except the garbage disposal, he proved he could do something right. She was very fond of Row right now. This was an unusual sensation for both of them. She would tell Mom, who would be thrilled to learn that this particular brother and sister had liked each other for five minutes.

"I flunked," said Row. "I wouldn't touch the dolls, either. But the instructor said that eventually a baby always stops crying. So now must be eventually." He sat on a big leather footstool, resting Sam on his lap, tiny feet against Row's stomach, head lying on his knees. Sam's mouth hung open and he breathed steadily and silently. "Fix me a bottle, Muff," said Row, "would you? Just in case he wakes up. I'll give him a late-night supper."

Dusty said, "Here's what. We just won't tell anybody anything, okay? Now, don't call your father, Kit. I'll just sort of camp here, okay? He won't come till the weekend, will he? I am sick of motels. I have more baby stuff in the trunk of the car, and this afternoon I stocked up on important things, like shampoo. I'll be fine, you won't have to worry about me at all, Kit."

Muffin pulled her features to the center of her face, lips, nose, eyebrows, and cheeks all meeting in a huge dramatic pout. "Nobody's worried about you, Dusty. The rest of us are worried about Sam the Baby."

At that moment, Kit Innes became a full person again. She was not dull and she was not calm, but she possessed some of those assets. She could think, even with the headache slamming against her skull. She needed facts. "Okay, Dusty," she said. "There's a lot more to this than you said to Row. You tell us the truth now, and don't you wiggle around and tell lies. Who exactly are Cinda and Burt? What are they afraid of? What are they running from? Why didn't they come to the hospital to get Sam? Why did you have to hide out in a motel? Who is Sam's father? You start talking, Dusty!"

Dusty burst into tears. "I don't know why you're being so hostile! I've had a terribly, terribly hard year, I was absolutely, utterly heartbroken when your father just walked away from our marriage, and dating again was so hard, and being pregnant was awful, and I had to work for Cinda and Burt, and I had to make so many decisions all by myself, and you just have to trust me. Cinda would be a wonderful mother, but they have problems. They're personal problems, and we can't get into them now, because it's none of your business. But I don't know why you have to be so mean about it. I don't know why people are always so mean."

Dusty did not actually have tears. She just had a tearful expression.

"Dusty, how can you stand there and not want to hold your baby?" said Muffin.

"I'm way too upset," said Dusty, "and Rowen is doing a wonderful job."

"Have you ever held Sam?" asked Muffin.

"Of course I've held him. That's not his name, though."

"What is his name?"

"Well, I didn't give him one, because Cinda and Burt were going to give him a name. But they — well — things started to go sour — and —" Dusty sank into a chair and covered her face with her hands.

Kit said, "Cinda and Burt were very upset that Muffin and I took pictures of them. They were so upset that Burt actually snatched my camera and put it in his car. What was that about? What were the things going sour?"

Dusty got up. She straightened her skirt and tugged a few locks of hair into different positions. "I don't think we ever talked about cameras," said Dusty. "Does anybody else want a Coke?"

"What do Cinda and Burt do for a living?" asked Kit.

"Who cares about that?" said Dusty, heading to the refrigerator. "They're not going to take the baby after all, so they don't matter."

"Dusty!" yelled Kit. "Answer me!"

"They're in computers. Banking. They make tons of money."

"They don't have furniture," said Muffin. "If you had tons of money, you'd have a table and chairs."

Dusty closed the fridge door without taking anything out. Maybe there wasn't anything in there to take out. "You see, Cinda and Burt are not going to leave me alone now! They gave me the money, so they expect to have the baby!"

"Then just give them back the money!" snapped Kit.

"I spent it. I spent a week at the casino and I bought some jewelry!" Dusty's face lit up remembering these treats.

"Who's the father?" Kit asked.

Dusty played with her hair.

"*Who is he?*"

"He isn't your father. He's a man I didn't even like. I thought it would make your father jealous. But Gavin didn't notice, he was back in California and never even knew, and I stopped going out with the man, because he was nothing compared to Gavin, but then it was too late, I was going to have his baby."

"You're dumb," said Muffin.

"You're only nine!" snapped Dusty. "You don't know how hard life is."

"You shouldn't go out of your way to make it harder," said Muffin.

"And where did you go, anyway, when you handed me your baby?" said Kit. "What was so important that you had to drive off like that? Don't lie to me. It's perfectly obvious what you did. You had your hair done! You had it colored! And set!"

Did Dad see into her one day, thought Kit, and understand that she possesses no affection or concern? She possesses only her demanding shallow self? Did he say, I have to get out of this? And then did I actually argue with him, saying, Dad, you have to be kind? Kit gagged.

"Why are you pestering me?" sobbed Dusty. "I don't know why you're being so cruel! Yes, I had my hair done! I could not go on looking as dreadful as I did. And I was going to find a place for the baby and me to live until I figured out what to do next. I had nowhere to live."

"Dusty," said Kit, "my father is paying for your apartment. So why do you need a place? It's there. And it's beautiful. Remember, I've seen it? Dad gave you the best."

"Well, actually I subleased the apartment and spent the summer working for Cinda and Burt."

"*Why?*"

"Because your father doesn't trust me with cash, and he drew up an alimony agreement where he pays bills, but I don't get cash, and that's not fair, Kit, it's just not fair, so I rented out the apartment to somebody else, and that's the money I'm living on, although it is not enough, he has just not been fair."

"So you stayed with Cinda and Burt?"

"Yes. But they — well, I really didn't like them very much. You see, Cinda and Burt were —"

"Witches," said Muffin.

"Exactly. So after the baby was born, I stayed in a motel, and put a rental car on my charge, but you can't take care of a baby in a motel room, and Burt and Cinda were just not collecting cash the way they expected to, and I needed a house and a kitchen. So I drove here, and I thought, Well, I'll just stay in this house because Gavin's out of town, and it's a perfectly fine house with everything in it but food, and I'll think things through, and I might even call Gavin and get some advice.

"And then you were here, Kit, and it was perfect! It was meant. And my strategy was to find an apartment. And of course there was shopping to do. And since it was you, there was nothing to worry about, and I looked terrible, so I had my hair done."

Kit could imagine this perfectly. Dusty driving around with her little mental list: orange juice, paper towels, hair salon.

But to anybody else, it was the list of a mental case. When you had a baby, the only thing on the list was the baby. Dusty should have stayed at the house with the baby while Kit ran the errands.

Kit could imagine Dusty *wanting* to be a decent mother, and remembering it occasionally. But she couldn't imagine Dusty actually *being* a decent mother.

Even now, it was Row cuddling the sleeping infant; Dusty was busy with explanations.

Not even explanations, now that Kit paid closer attention.

Blame. Dusty was blaming other people for this position she was in: Dad had divorced her; the unnamed man got her pregnant; Ed cornered her; giving birth was more upsetting than she'd thought and might ruin her looks; and now Kit was giving her a hard time.

Sam slept on. Rowen gently shifted Sam into the very spot where Kit had had him, the cleft in the back of the sofa, where he lay comfortably and safely on his back. The beautiful shelf clock on the enormous chimney mantel chimed nine. Kit was stunned. All this had happened and it was only nine o'clock?

What a lottery it was, having a parent! Here was Sam, beautiful perfect Sam (except when he was crying) (or having diarrhea), and his mother was an unthinking selfish stupid mess. If Dusty kept Sam, poor Sam's life would be a string of careless sitters and a glamorous mother shopping or going to the casino.

Kit thought of Julie, whose mother was alcoholic and foul-mouthed; Ellie, whose mother was alcoholic but hid it well, and spent her life shut up in the house; David, whose parents hit him; Shelby, whose parents had never seen their champion daughter play field hockey, never shown up at a teacher conference to hear what a wonderful student she was, never came to the play for which Shelby had designed sets.

So many friends had lost the parent lottery.

I don't want Sam in that lottery, thought Kit. But he's there already, and I don't know how to take him out of it.

"Okay," said Rowen, "so Ed is also getting paid fifty thousand, to deliver the baby. He's committing a crime, I'm sure of that. Well, no, actually I have no idea whether New Jersey has statutes about baby selling, but it feels like a crime. I say we call the police right now, and —"

"No, no, no!" shouted Dusty. She smacked her hand down on the counter. "You can't accuse Ed of a crime! He's my cousin and I said it was all right to do it, and anyway it would get me in trouble, too."

Muffin wanted them to shut up. Who cared about Dusty's stupid life? Even though Row had had the baby on his lap, and even though Kit was doing her best, it seemed to Muffin that the baby was not coming first here.

We should make a list, thought Muffin, whose mother never moved without several lists. The baby needs milk and more baby wipes. He needs clothes and another blanket. He needs a mattress with a sheet that has Winnie-the-Poohs on it. He can't spend his life propped up on people's shoulders.

"Let's go home, Row," she said. "Mom will know what to do. Our old crib is still in the attic. I know because I play dolls in it."

But nobody heard her.

The doorbell was ringing. Dusty got to the door first, and let in Ed Bing.

Chapter 10

"Don't be mad, Eddie," said Dusty. She led her cousin into the family room as if he were royalty. "We can fix things up, don't you worry."

"Fix things up?" said Kit. She had topped out on the day's events. She could not spend another second listening to Dusty's excuses and nonsense. She pointed to Sam. "You can't fix that up. He was born. He has a stupid mother. We're calling the police."

"No, Kit!" whispered Dusty. "Don't you understand? I can't be in that much trouble!"

"Dusty, how much trouble can you be in? You changed your mind about an adoption."

"Then we don't need police, do we?" said Ed, trying to smile. "Kit, I feel as if I've done everything wrong. I was only trying to help."

"He was only trying to help," agreed Dusty.

Ed looked at Rowen much as he had tried to look into the house that afternoon, looking around and sort of behind him, as if trying to figure out just who this boy was, and how much to worry about him. Rowen said, "I'm Muffin's brother. I've been baby-sitting for Sam here."

"Sam?" said Ed.

"The baby," explained Dusty. "They've been calling him Sam."

Everybody turned to look at the baby. He lay under a dish towel with a pattern of forks along the edge. He was quite beautiful, and so small, to fit beneath such a little piece of cloth.

"Look," said Ed, "Cinda and Burt have arranged this wonderful adoption, and they're moving out of state to new jobs, and they've shipped the furniture on ahead to the new house, and then Dusty backed out! Naturally Cinda and Burt stayed on in their empty house, trying to smooth things over and still get their darling baby boy. You're right, Muffin, they were out of soap. But that's because they expected to be a thousand miles away by now. They're nice people, Muffin, and they don't usually have pizza every night and they don't usually run out of soap. They took care of Dusty during her pregnancy, and when she gave birth, Dusty just panicked." Ed turned to his cousin and smiled at her. "But you feel better now, don't you? Let's take the baby to Cinda and Burt. You know why they're in such a hurry, Dusty. They have to start their new jobs and they just can't indefinitely wait here for you to calm down."

It sounded logical to Row. His sister often drove him crazy, and he could imagine her charging perfectly nice people with being witches. He certainly didn't want poor Sam raised by Dusty. Row spent a minute feeling grateful for his own mother. Mom had her flaws, but an extra-high interest in green vegetables was a better flaw than Dusty's.

For the first time, Dusty picked her baby up. Rowen was relieved to see that she did this carefully and gently, and kissed his little bald head, and moved him slowly so he wouldn't wake up. He imagined getting fifty thousand dollars, like Dusty and Ed. He'd always dreamed of having his own race car — not a cheap hobby — which meant Row could spend his fifty thou in one place in one day.

How would Sam feel, one day, when Sam was older, maybe Rowen's own age, and his adoptive parents explained to him that he had cost a hundred thousand dollars? What if my parents had bought me? thought Rowen.

It was creepy, way beyond the creepy of Halloween witches.

On the other hand, a couple that saved up a hundred thousand in order to have a baby was a couple who really wanted that baby, and certainly Dusty didn't want him. So maybe this was a good thing.

But Cinda and Burt had not come up with the cash.

"None of this is actually your business, Kit," said Dusty. She sounded grown-up all of a sudden. She'd been a whining teenager, an incompetent driver, and a thirsty guest, but she had definitely not been an adult.

"Dusty," said Row, "what was it about Cinda and Burt that made you change your mind? I think that's important. We should discuss that."

"Rowen," said Dusty, "even though you are cute and I love your clothes, you are not the mother of this baby and we will have no more discussion. This is a case of everybody misunderstanding everybody else. I got very excited, in fact I got hysterical. You know me, Kit, you know this is my history. I am very fragile, and emotional upsets are very very very difficult for me to handle. I see now that I cannot be a successful mother, because I'm far too fragile. But the very best thing, Kit, is for me to stay here, and in the morning I will telephone your father. I certainly know how angry he will be, but I know I can count on his advice. He is very levelheaded."

And rich, thought Row. Maybe even willing to come up with a check, as big as the one Cinda and Burt were supposed to deliver, just to get you out of his house.

"Kit, be a sweet, sweet girl," said Dusty, "and get me a baby blanket. There are flannel sheets upstairs in the linen closet. I bought them, so I know they're there. Get the blue flat sheet."

"It's a twin bed sheet for my room," protested Kit. "It would wrap a dozen babies."

"Cut it down," said Dusty. "Or fold it up."

"Anyway," said Muffin, with her pouty glare, "it isn't your sheet anymore, Dusty. This isn't a hotel, and even if it was a hotel, you couldn't go around stealing sheets."

The baby's legs twitched, moving the tea towel an inch. It was enough to bare his skin and make the rest of them shiver.

"Okay," said Kit, thinking that blue flannel was nice, actually. A boy color for a little boy who hadn't had anything yet. There were scissors in the bathroom, which she used for cutting the price tags off new clothes. She could cut the sheet in two, or in four.

"Which room are you going to stay in, Dusty?" she asked. "I read once, maybe it was in Laura Ingalls Wilder, about using a bureau drawer for a baby basket. I'll get a drawer and line it with the rest of the flannel sheet and that will be the baby's bed."

Dusty clapped. "Kit, you are so bright. I would never have thought of that."

Rowen heard sarcasm in Dusty's voice, and he was slightly surprised. He would not have thought Dusty was smart enough to be sarcastic.

"I'll stay in the guest room," she said, "where I used to keep my dolls."

Dolls? thought Rowen. He had a lot of questions to ask Kit. He darted up the stairs after her, to mutter his questions quickly where Dusty wouldn't overhear. The house was enormous. The linen "closet" was a room.

"Are you okay with this, Kit?" he said, catching up to her.

"I don't know. I don't know what to do and I don't know what not to do. But waitning till tomorrow to hear what Dad has to say — I'm okay on that. Actually, I know the hotel he's going to stay in tonight, he's in Seattle, and I think I'll just stay here instead of Shea's, and I'll keep calling Seattle, and —"

Muffin came racing up the stairs. "Row! Kit! Row!"

"What?"

"They're leaving," said Muffin. "They left. They took Sam and they left. They're driving away."

They pounded down the stairs and flung themselves at the door.

Ed was just pulling away. He actually grinned at them, honking good-bye and leaving a patch as he tore out of the cul-de-sac.

"We're following them," said Row.

"Yes!" said Muffin.

"What for?" said Kit, fighting tears. "Dusty is Sam's mother. She does get to choose where she takes her baby. If she chooses Ed, or Cinda, or another motel, that's her choice, isn't it? We can't even call the police. It's her baby."

Row felt shivery. He hadn't learned much in 'Boy, Oh, Boy — Babies!' but he had learned one thing. You had to put them first, the way his parents had certainly always put him and Muff first. And now Dusty was driving off. "Did she take the car seat?" he said to Muffin.

"No. She's holding him. And she didn't put her seat belt on, either."

Rowen turned to Kit, and immediately knew that she just wanted them out of the house. The whole thing was so unpleasant, so hard to understand, and Sam's little life looked so difficult — Row was abruptly embarrassed that he had trepassed on this nasty little soap opera episode of her father's divorce.

He watched the car turn left.

The golf course development had only one real exit; Ed had to leave by one particular road. He'd turned the wrong way, and would have to wander down another dead end before he got himself facing out again.

"I'm staying here, and I'm calling my father," said Kit.

"We'll keep in touch," said Row, moving

his little sister toward the door. "Keep the house locked. I'll call from Shea's, okay?"

Kit nodded.

His sister took his hand, which surprised him. Muff must be feeling as sick over this as he was. He squeezed her fingers gently and she squeezed back. They went to his car and got in and belted up and he started the engine and Muffin said, "Row? Do you think Sam the Baby will be okay?"

He couldn't bear to tell his baby sister how far from okay Sam's life looked. His eyes were racing, trying to find Ed. They couldn't be far ahead. He'd been counting seconds in his head; forty seconds had passed since Ed had turned the wrong way.

"Did you have any supper, Muff?" he said casually.

"No."

"Want to stop at McDonald's before we go to Aunt Karen's?"

"Yes." Muffin loved Happy Meals. She had saved every single toy from every single one she'd ever had.

Row scanned all traffic, all everything, and then he doused his headlights and waited on the cul-de-sac, unmoving, invisible, his little sister not noticing what he had just done, because she was thinking about her Happy Meal. Ed Bing came out of the wrong cul-de-sac and drove right in front of Row, and Rowen Mason was hot with triumph: He could follow them.

Part of his mind said: What do you think you're doing? Part of his mind said: Way cool. Following cars! Part of his mind said: I'm starving, too. Hope we do pass a McDonald's.

He turned on the radio. A person needed music to follow by. Naturally he got news.

Ed and Dusty stopped at Dunkin' Donuts and a moment later, Ed was driving along with a cruller in his left hand and a large coffee in his right. This slowed him down. Dusty was sitting in the passenger seat with the baby on her shoulder, a coffee in one hand, and no shoulder strap visible. It occurred to Row that Ed might never have installed seat belts; the Caddy was so old it had not come with them.

There was one car between Row and the Caddy. Neither Ed nor Dusty would notice Rowen and Muffin. They were not the types to check rearview mirrors.

The divided road became an intersection with so many turn lanes you would expect the choices of destination to be Washington, D.C., and New York; but it was just a regular old crossroad, and Rowen, instead of staying in the center lane and heading for Aunt Karen's, lined up behind Ed in the outside left turn lane.

Muffin said, "Are we following them? Good. Let's take Sam back. I think we should adopt him, Row. Don't you think Mom would be a good mommy for Sam?"

Row tried to imagine himself bringing a baby home for his mother to raise. He said, "I don't know, Muff. I think Mom may have other plans for her life."

"What are we doing, then?"

"I don't know. I'm just doing it. It's cool, and what can happen?"

The light changed.

Ed stuck his cruller in his mouth and turned left using one palm and the edge of the coffee cup. Row had to follow; all New Jersey would honk at him if he delayed a split second.

"Where does this road go?" Muffin asked her brother. "Do you think we're going to pass a McDonald's? I was going to order at Dunkin' Donuts, but then you never really drove in. I'm starving, Row. I still say we should call 911."

The road started out four lanes, narrowed quickly to two, and left behind the stores and the lights. Rowen's mind flitted around like his sister's, from food to baby to 911 to left turns. He was crawling with unease. It reminded him of a truly awful sweat suit his mother had acquired: plain gray fleece, but covered with a sprinkling of ants! They were extremely well drawn, so that you wanted to rush up to her and brush her off. Row's skin felt like that, and his brain. He needed to brush himself off.

"This is so stupid," he said to his sister. "I have absolutely no idea what we are doing this for."

"We love Sam," said Muffin.

Rowen had let quite a bit of distance get between himself and Ed because even Ed might sense something odd about this car on his tail; even Dusty might turn and recognize them. He thought he would just let the distance increase and increase, until he could not distinguish the old Caddy anymore, and then they would turn around and go by way of McDonald's to his cousin's, and from there he would call Kit and make sure she was okay.

He had the bad guy in his headlights, so she had to be okay.

Way up ahead of them, Ed pulled his Caddy over onto the shoulder of the road.

It was a vacant stretch. No stores; no houses.

Rowen thought Ed was going to swing a

U-ie and go back to the main road; probably Ed had taken a wrong turn here, busy with doughnuts and arguing. Rowen, too, slowed down, and then put out his headlights, so Ed wouldn't notice the car idling behind him, and came to a full stop. He was pretty far away. Maybe the length of a football field. Rowen would wait for them to make a U-turn, and then he would, too, but he and Muffin would go to McDonald's and then to Shea's, because this was lasting too long and he was sick of feeling sick about it.

Dusty, baby in arms, got out of the car.

She opened the back door. She set the baby in the back.

Muffin cried out, "Row! She doesn't have the car seat, she's just setting him there! If Ed brakes hard, Sam will fly up into the air and go through the windshield!"

Because Ed's car doors were open, the interior lights were on, and Dusty was a clear silhouette in the night. Row lowered his window and turned down the radio. Across the long distance, he could hear Sam, crying steadily.

Dusty stepped back from the car and then closed the rear door.

"She's sick of holding him," whispered

Muffin. "He's crying and she doesn't want to hold him when he cries."

Ed drove away.

He drove away while Dusty was still outside the car.

Dusty screamed.

Ed slammed the accelerator to the floor and his car spurted forward, tires screaming. The passenger door, still open for Dusty to get back in, looked as if it would just snap off, but from the leaning of the car as Ed speeded up, it slammed itself shut.

Row had been right about the U-turn.

Ed was leaving Dusty on the side of the road and driving back the way he had come with the baby.

Dusty was running after the Caddy, screaming and shrieking.

Ed floored the accelerator.

Oh my God, thought Rowen. The baby isn't fastened to anything! He isn't safe in anything! He's just lying on the seat.

But probably not now.

By now he would have fallen to the floor, and in what position? Where was his little mouth? What about his little neck? Where had his little head hit?

Ed raced past them going back the way

they had come. In seconds he would be out of sight. Rowen put on his headlights, slammed his foot to the floor, and followed Ed in a tire-screaming turn.

"What about Dusty?" shrieked Muffin.

"She can take care of herself," said Rowen. "Why don't we have a car phone? What are we going to do? Ed's going to hurt Sam."

Muffin put the strap of her seat belt in her mouth and chewed on it, a habit for which Muff was always getting screamed at. Row didn't scream. He'd like to bite something himself right now.

"We can't lose Ed, Row!" said his sister, beginning to cry. "You've got to stick to him. We'll catch him, we'll call the police, we should have called 911 already, we were wrong to decide everything was okay, he's kidnapping the baby now, plus he's going to hurt Sam."

Row did not know how he was going to contact the police at the same time he had to stay on Ed's tail.

CHAPTER 11

As soon as Muffin and Rowen were out of the driveway, Kit picked up the phone to call her father. What a relief it would be to hear his sturdy decisive voice. She did hear his sturdy decisive voice. Unfortunately, it was his answering machine.

"Dad," she said onto the tape, "call me at your house. It's an emergency with Dusty."

She shouldn't have said that. Everything was an emergency with Dusty. Dad would cringe and not call, hoping Dusty's emergency (a grass stain on her tennis skirt, perhaps) would solve itself.

So she called back and left a second message. "Really, Dad, you've got to call me. The situation is extremely serious. It involves her cousin Ed and a baby-selling scheme. They're terrified of the police and I think something else is going on. I believe the baby is in danger. Call me, Dad!"

She left messages everywhere she could, including the Seattle hotel.

Then she called Mom and Malcolm and got their answering machine.

Oh, good grief! thought Kit as there was another series of knocks on the front door. She set the phone down and ran to the door, calling, "Who is it?" and Muffin said in her high flute voice, "It's me, Muffin!" and Kit opened the door.

It was easy to tell which car was Ed's. His right red rear light had been damaged and not repaired, so a streak of white zapped through the broken red glass. Ed went back to the divided road and took the entrance ramp to Route 80.

"We're going to Cinda and Burt's," said Muffin. "Kit and I drove here already. He's delivering Sam. I even know what exit to take."

Row passed a semi and a Jaguar.

"We don't have to drive this fast," said his sister, thus losing her status as a sweet little kid after all and becoming a nag.

He didn't lift his foot from the gas. It was fun. He'd never even approached this speed. He was actually chasing a car, in the dark of night, in the thick of traffic. No parent, no aunt, no cousin knew where he was, and nobody could tell him what to do. Especially not his nine-year-old sister.

"If you hit somebody, we're grease spots on the road," said Muffin. This was a frequent comment of their mother's when Dad drove above the speed limit.

Eighty miles an hour was a quick way to cover ground.

In no time, Ed was on an exit ramp, and Muffin was saying she and Kit had already been here today, and they went a mile here, a mile there, so deep in the country that Rowen could not imagine how he'd find his way home. They flew by a twenty-four-hour convenience store (convenient to whom? Nobody lived here!), but he hardly had time to mark it on a mental map and they were on another road.

He lost Ed.

The car was just gone.

The road was straight and empty.

He slowed down, listening to crickets. He could hear no engine but his own.

Muffin said, "This is the turn. Right

here, Row. Go through where that fence is broken."

Burt and Cinda were in the house before Kit could stop them, locking her door behind them and separating, so that Burt was between Kit and the rest of her house, and Cinda was between Kit and the door.

The extent of her stupidity struck her like a slap. Over and over she had had a chance to do what Muffin wanted to do: Call 911. Over and over, Dusty had said, You don't know how much trouble I'm in. Over and over, Kit had not listened.

Cinda had imitated Muffin's voice. Piped out a high-pitched lie to get in the door. That was not how you adopted a baby! That was not how you did anything, ever, at all!

Cinda and Burt were so ordinary-looking. They had ordinary glasses and ordinary features. But they had been knocked out of the ordinary. They were crazy.

"Please get out of my house," said Kit. If she had ever needed her Dullness Training, it was now, but she had lost it. Terror collapsed her voice like a old tent, and they knew it.

"The baby," said Cinda, trying to smile.

She held out her hands and turned her wrists at angles, as if an invisible baby lay cradled there. "We've changed our minds. We can still take the baby. You need to understand that I have waited for this baby for so long, and I had never seen him, after all that waiting, and he was so beautiful, and you drove away, and that wasn't fair after all! We did arrange to have him! He really is ours. So I've come for my son. Our son. We're taking him with us."

"The camera," said Burt softly. "We'll take the camera, too."

"I don't have the camera," said Kit, "and I don't have Sam."

"No!" said Burt, grabbing her arm and shaking it. "We have to have it! You get it for us!"

I have to slow them down, thought Kit. Either get explanations or get them out. What do I do? What do I offer, since I don't have the baby or the camera?

At Mom's there would be food. Mom believed in food. Food helped with new neighbors, funerals, arguments, celebrations — and, presumably, craziness.

"No," whimpered Cinda. "No, I know you have the baby. You were taking such good care of him, I know he's here, I know we got lost trying to find you, but we did find you, and I know you have the baby. Please, please, he's my baby."

"How about a cup of tea?" said Kit, although there were no tea bags, no sugar, and no lemon. But if she could get into the kitchen by herself, she could run out the back, disappear into the dark of the golf course, and surface on another road — namely, her own — and call the police.

"I only drink herbal tea," said Cinda. "What kinds do you have?"

"Stop it!" said Burt. "Cinda, don't be a jerk. We're not here for refreshments! We have to get that camera film."

"I am not a jerk! The whole thing was your idea, anyway. I just went along with it. I didn't know —"

Burt smacked her.

The sound of his flat hand against Cinda's cheek and mouth was a sound Kit had never heard before. She had never seen a woman stagger back from being hit. Never seen the shock that crossed Cinda's face; nor the acceptance. And she had certainly never seen that amount of fury; the fury on Burt's face.

Kit was paralyzed. Her tongue could not fold itself around any words whatsoever. It lay there and she stood there.

"Where's the camera?" said Burt to Kit.

He was not armed. There was no weapon. But he was dangerous. He was panicky, angry, tired, and, she realized now, stupid. Stupid like Dusty. Stupid people did stupid things. They were stupid to have come here, stupid to have followed her, stupid to have locked the door.

But she had something in common with Cinda and Burt now. Fear.

Kit had to get away from the topic of the camera, because she had no way to hand over that camera.

Or did she?

There was the stack of disposable cameras on the counter. Of course, they were still in boxes, never having been used. Could she get into the kitchen, unwrap a camera, take ten pictures of the floor, and bring the camera out as if those had been the ones Muffin took of the baby?

"The camera!" said Burt.

He was going to slap Kit now.

She fought her way to calm. Calm had always been something below her; something easily reached; something she sort of lay down on, like a nap. It was odd to have to leap and stretch for calm, as if it were way above, on a cliff edge, crumbling under her curled fingers. "You know, Burt, Muff and I went to your house. We know you and Cinda now, and we know where you live. So, I guess I don't understand what difference pictures make. I mean, so what if there's film? There are witnesses."

"Where is my baby?" said Cinda, in a broken voice. "We always knew it was a risk, adopting privately like this, but Dusty was so much fun at first. She did her share. And we were going to have enough money to pay for the baby. It should have worked. Dusty and I did all the ATMs and —"

"Cinda!" said her husband.

Cinda kept pressing her lips together, and then separating them, and pressing them back down, as if they itched. "Well, we did! I've always wanted a baby, Kit, and Burt and I went through that fertility stuff at the clinic and neither one of us can have a baby, can you believe it, Kit, what are the odds of that? Two healthy people and neither one —"

"Cinda," said Burt.

"— but it's not okay, not having my son. I did buy clothes for him, whatever that little girl Muffin said! They're packed in my Cherokee. I have a mobile to hang over his crib, it sings 'Winnie-the-Pooh.' " She sang the four notes of that song: "*Winnie-the-Pooh, Winnie-the-Pooh.*"

Okay, great, thought Kit, Cinda just

went over the edge. I cannot join her. I have to enter my Dullness Training. Reentry. That's what I'm after here; one of us has got to stay sane. Or run like hell. "Now, the camera, Burt. It's in the kitchen, actually."

"Get it."

Oh, good! This was going to be easy, then! She'd saunter off to the kitchen, race out the back door, vanish onto the golf course —

But Burt took her arm in his hand. It was a small hand, for a man. And strong. The fingers that had just slapped Cinda so hard now closed with equal force just above her elbow, and crunched. He did not seem to know he was holding her so tightly. His breath was coming in tight little spurts, and his fingers clenched and unclenched.

Kit achieved dullness. "What are you guys doing out there in the country, anyway?" she said cheerfully. "Raising marijuana? It's a good location." She nodded, so they would understand that she understood. "You're probably growing it underground in tunnels or deep in the woods, aren't you? Listen, I won't tell."

Burt began to cry. Except on television or in movies, Kit had never seen a man cry.

Burt had no experience in crying. His cheeks, mouth, and eyes were distorted, unaccustomed to this kind of twitch.

They reached the family room, with its chilly huge furnishings, and the kitchen, with its pile of disposable cameras. There was no way to pretend that one of them had been used and somehow climbed back into its foil and its cardboard.

Kit said, "You'll find another baby someday, Cinda." She hoped not. She hoped a social worker would say, These nutcases? A baby? Never!

She had reentered dullness, and in the calm of her mind, words here and there began surfacing, like letters on a Scrabble board, and she began arranging them on her mental Scrabble rack.

Kit had a shivery sense of knowledge just out of reach: A little fact was frisking over to the side; if she sat still, and let her mind drift, she could rope the fact in. It was from television, she had heard it on *New Jersey News*, back when she was afraid that Dusty might have kidnapped Sam the Baby. What had the other news been? Stocks had been up. A power plant was having minor but meaningful failures. State police were closer to solving a rash of—

Letters spurted out her mouth.

She could feel them coming, she tried to stop them, tried to fold her tongue up again, but the letters came out anyway. "ATM," she said. "It's you, isn't it?" Understanding spread over her face like peanut butter on bread. "You're the ones! The police are after you. That's why you're out of time."

Burt let her go. In order to slap her? To run away from what she was saying? Or to cover his eyes and weep some more?

"And that's what's on the camera, isn't it?" said Kit. "Your license plates. Neither one of them is New Jersey. With those plate numbers, the police will know what your real names are; in what town and state you really live. You won't be able to vanish."

Burt's eyes glittered at Kit's.

But with Cinda, it was not eyes that glittered.

She had entered Dad's useless kitchen. She had found something. The decorator had forgotten no detail; he had prepared the room for cooking.

Cinda had a knife.

It was a rutted, rarely used lane, very narrow, gravel thrown into the worst potholes. Quite literally, Rowen could not back out now. It was way too long and curving a road for him to manage for such a great distance. There was no grass at the edge, the gravel went straight into trees; there was no room to turn around.

The car antenna whipped in the snares of branches.

"Turn off your headlights," whispered Muffin.

Her whispering gave him the creeps.

"They're not far now. The woods stop in a little bit. And the driveway has a big loop in it so you don't have to turn."

His baby sister knew he was afraid of backing up; or had observed his lousy backing. Who else knew?

He obeyed her instructions and soon there was black flatness, probably the yard, and a house that was just a dark splat against a dark sky. There were no lights.

He whispered back, "This can't be it! If Ed came here, Muff, we'd —"

A car door slammed. It was definitely a car door; it had the metal *thwonk* that house doors did not. But he could see no car. Where was Ed? Why was it entirely dark? Had he turned off his interior lights so there would be no illumination when he opened his doors?

Then, the raw angry cry of a baby.

"If Sam can cry like that, he isn't really hurt," said Muffin, relaxing.

Or he's very, very hurt, thought Rowen.

Rowen and Muffin sat motionless in the dark of their own car, peering blindly into the dark that was full of sound.

A minute passed.

Inside the house, lights went on in a large room with good-sized windows. These cast a little light into the yard, enough to see Ed's car near the front door. Inside, Ed held the baby.

"Cinda and Burt aren't here," whispered Muffin. "The driveway is empty. Their two cars were here before. They have Grand Cherokees."

"I don't want to yank Sam out of Ed's arms," murmured Rowen. "Ed is nuts. He's thinking of his money. If there's no adoption, he doesn't get the rest of his cash. He's going to make this adoption work or else. I can turn around on the grass, and hope Ed doesn't see us. Or back up into the meadow and hope there's no ditch to get hung up on. Then we'll go to that convenience store and use their phone to call the police. You were right, Muff. We should have done that in the first place." Rowen put the car into reverse.

"I'm not leaving," said Muffin. "I'm going to go in and help Ed with the baby. Look at Ed. He's getting really mad at Sam for screaming."

Ed was flailing his arms around as if directing a junior high band. He did not look like a baby-sitter. He looked like a baby hater.

If only I had a car phone! thought Rowen.

He could leave his car in the narrow track, blocking Ed's exit, while he ran the mile back to make the phone call. But it was much more than a mile to the convenience store. That was not sensible. Besides, Ed wouldn't be going anywhere. He was at the place he'd meant to go to. They didn't have to worry that he'd drive off before the police got here.

Muffin touched her door handle.

"No!" said her brother. "You may not go in there! The guy is nuts!"

"What if he hurts the baby?"

"I don't think he'll hurt the baby," said Rowen, who was sure that Ed would hurt the baby unless his luck changed very soon. "He wants his money. He's waiting for Cinda and Burt to come back. I think he'll just walk away from Sam and let him scream."

"I have a plan," said Muffin. "I'll crouch down by those bushes over there. I saw them in the daylight. They're plain old bushes and there's a cute little wire bench next to it. It's a good place. I'll watch and make sure he doesn't hurt the baby or leave. You drive away and get help."

"Don't be a jerk," said Rowen. "Do you know what Mom and Dad would do to me if I left my sister with a kidnapper in the woods? I'd be a paraplegic in the morning."

Muffin opened her window the whole way. "I'm not using the door, so the car lights won't go on." She stuck her head and chest out the window, sat on the window, twisted up her knees, and dropped to the ground.

"Get back in this car!" hissed Rowen.

"I am not leaving Sam. You go get the police. You go right now, Rowen!"

In the house, Ed moved to another room, and the baby was not in his arms. Since there was no furniture, he must have set Sam on the floor. At least Sam couldn't fall off anything. But he must be starving. And scared. Did a new baby know enough to be scared? Or was a new baby just feeling crummy and couldn't do a thing about it except yell?

"Muffin, you get in this car!"

Their furious whispers probably wouldn't carry across the field — but they might.

Ed came out the side door.

Rowen froze. His sister was out on the grass someplace, and Ed was — *getting into his car.*

But he didn't have the baby. The baby was still inside.

Rowen had never played a sport or taken an exam with so much he did not comprehend. He could not imagine what he was supposed to do. He got out of the car because he had to confront Ed in some way.

If he'd had an hour to think, or even a minute, Row would have realized that a confrontation with Ed could only end badly; that Ed had lost the ability to think clearly; that for Ed to leave the baby alone was actually a good thing, because Row and Muffin could take Sam back.

But Row didn't have time to think. It seemed necessary to get out of his car, quickly, and prevent Ed from driving away. Row walked forward in the dark, and Ed put the heavy powerful Cadillac into gear and drove right into him.

The huge knife gleamed in Cinda's hand.

Burt stepped far away from his wife.

Kit had nowhere to step.

The telephone rang.

It jolted them badly.

It's Dad, thought Kit. He's calling me back.

Burt and Cinda were trying to see where the phone was. There was at least one phone in every room. But the decorator found telephones and television screens unattractive and had hidden them.

"It's my father," said Kit in her friendliest voice. "He's checking on me. If I don't answer and the machine gets it, he'll know there's something wrong."

The phone rang a second time.

"Your father's in California," said Cinda. "You think we don't know everything about this house? Dusty talked about Gavin Innes and this place and that golf course and you all the time."

A third ring and the answering machine picked up.

"Kits Bits," said her father. He was using an old old nickname; age three was when he called her Kits Bits. "I'm sorry Dusty appeared again."

Cinda took Kit's wrist and held it in a contemplative fashion, deciding whether to slash it crosswise or vertically.

Dad said, "Dusty is not as simple as she appears, Kit. She's a manipulative woman, extraordinarily selfish, and I want you to be very careful of being drawn into her net. *She* should not be at that house, and *you* should not be at that house. I called your mother and Malcolm, but they're not home, and now you're not at our house, so I'm calling the police to get right over to the house and see what's going on." He disconnected.

The word *police* jarred Cinda.

For a moment she was simply bewildered, as if lost in a large parking lot. She released her hold on Kit. The knife sagged in her fingers. It was a large steel knife, the kind television chefs used to chop up an onion faster than most people could even locate the chopping board.

Kit did not move. There was nowhere to go.

"The police," whispered Cinda. "Oh, Burt, how did we get into this? I don't want to go to jail. I'm not the kind of person who goes to jail. I'm a nice person. I don't want this to be happening."

"Well, it is happening," said Burt. "And I remember every one of Dusty's stories about this Gavin Innes. He will call the police and they will get here. You're coming with us," he said to Kit, and he took her arm once more, his fingers and thumb tightening like five bolts, fastening her to his side.

CHAPTER 12

When Ed walked outside of the house, all Muffin could think of was that Sam was indoors alone.

Muffin hated being alone in the house. She didn't care what time of day it was, she couldn't stand an empty house. She would visit neighbors she didn't like; she would sit on the steps outside in the rain; she would go with her mother on the most annoying errand; but she would not stay alone in the house.

Sam, who was new, was alone in the house. It wasn't even a real house. It was trash and paper thrown around, but no pillows and blankets and bottles of milk.

Ed got into his car.

Muffin could not believe it. He was going to drive away. And Sam, poor Sam, must be lying on the floor! And he didn't even have a shirt on, he was still in his tea towel, with its pattern of forks! Kit hadn't even gotten the blue blanket piece down the stairs before Dusty and Ed drove away.

Ed started his engine.

Ed was not the type to look behind him. Muffin leaped up from her crouch on the dark grass, ran to the front steps, and turned the handle of the front door. It was locked. "Why, you creep!" she whispered, meaning Ed. How was she supposed to get in to take care of Sam the Baby?

She tiptoed among the little button-top foundation shrubs to look in the windows and see where Sam was crying, but they were too high for her. She couldn't see in.

Ed drove off with the kind of spurt that would leave trenches in the driveway.

Muffin raced to the side door she remembered from her bathroom trip, holding her spread fingers in front of her face to ward off bugs and spiders and spiderwebs and bats. The door was unlocked.

It was a good thing she'd been to the bathroom here and checked everything out. Ed had left the light on where Sam was, but everything else was dark. She steered over half-remembered boxes and trash piles. "I'm coming, Sam," she called.

He was soaked with spit-up, and red from crying. Muffin scooped him up and crooned, "Poor, poor, poor, poor, poor Sam the Baby. But I'm here now. We'll tell on Ed. We'll tell my mother he left you alone in a house in the dark. We'll tell the police."

Telling Mom was much more serious than telling police.

Outside, it sounded as if Ed had hit a tree.

"Everything is fine, Sam," she told him, but Sam did not believe her. Which showed he was smarter than his mother, Dusty. Because everything was not fine.

She used toilet paper to mop his runny nose and dropped his used diaper on the floor, because there was no place else to put it, and dried him with toilet paper, and folded up the tea towel for a diaper. She had nothing to fasten it with, so she held it together with her hands.

Then she began hunting for a telephone. Ed had to have driven out the driveway by this time, so she turned on the lights. She found the jack in the kitchen, but no phone was hooked up. There was a sweater draped over an open cabinet door and Muffin examined it carefully. It belonged to a grown-up man. It was a button-up-the-front kind and it was old and snarly. It would have to do for Sam the Baby. She wrapped him in it, tying the sleeves around him twice, and he was easier to hold when he was tucked in and fastened like that, and it felt less likely that he would just skid out of her arms.

She found a jack in the living room, but no phone was hooked up to that, either.

The house had no telephone.

Rowen picked himself up off the grass, grateful for years of athletic events in which he had learned to avoid being crushed or caught. He'd turned his ankle, but he was good at limping until the shock wore off; you did that in a game; you didn't surrender to the injury, you got back into play.

He staggered into the shadows on the far side of the drive and tried to be a tree. He didn't think Ed had even seen him. Ed was so frantic to be out of here, he'd started without bothering to flick on his headlights. He'd been going five or ten miles an hour and wasn't looking. It hadn't occurred to him there was anything to look for. Well, it hadn't occurred to Rowan in his plan to stop Ed that Ed wouldn't see him standing there in the grass, saying, No, don't leave. But it was dark and shadowed, and Ed was fiddling with the dashboard, and Row had flung himself to the side.

Then Ed put on his lights.

Then there turned out to be a car parked in his way — Rowen's — and Ed's passenger side scraped hard along the driver's side of Rowen's car. Ed didn't react fast, and drove all the way down both cars before stopping.

Rowen cringed at the thought of the damage to his car. He wasn't even going to think about what his parents would say.

Where was Muffin? Row couldn't see her. "Muff!" he stage-whispered. She didn't answer.

In the faint light from the front room of the house, he spotted her peering in windows.

Muffin! he thought.

Ed backed up. He wasn't going to leave now that he knew a trespasser was here. Row decided to stay in the shadows until Ed got back out of his car, and then tackle him; immobilize Ed so he couldn't hurt Muff or the baby. Then Row and Muff and the baby would get out of here. His car would drive fine, it was just bashed up.

But Ed drove in a circle and launched his vehicle straight into Rowen's. He hit Row's car like a race driver passing on the inside turn, not caring about scrapes and dents. Their two sides collided with a horrible mangling of metals and when Ed made a huge U-turn in the grass, Rowen realized that Ed was going to make a third pass at Rowen's car; he was going to have his own personal demolition derby out here in the yard.

Rowen raced to the house to get Muffin and Sam. He ignored his aching ankle.

But Ed was not making a third run at Rowen's car.

He drove over the lawn, reaching the side door before Rowen did, leaped out of the car, and ran into the house in which Muffin had turned on every ceiling light.

Muffin, holding Sam in his sweater, was in the kitchen.

If Muffin had been alone, she would have been terrified. But she was not alone. She had Sam. He was a burden, really; six or eight pounds of hunger and thirst. But Sam could not live without her. She had gotten him clean, she had gotten him warm, and now she was going to get him fed. Ed was not important, the way he would have been if Muffin had been alone.

Muffin glared at Ed. "You're going to be in a whole lot of trouble. My brother Rowen is driving to the store to use the phone. He's calling the police. So there." Muffin made a hug of herself, with Sam tucked inside her crossed arms. She could feel his tiny heart beat against her ribs.

"Give me that camera," said Ed, a demand that startled her completely. Muffin had forgotten the camera. So that was the annoying, hard rectangle pressed against her belly button, getting in the way of holding Sam. "You can have it," she said. "But I have to keep holding Sam."

"You do that." Ed's fat hand, its fingernails split and stained, reached down to her tummy as he took the camera out of her kangaroo pouch. "Don't drop the baby, Muffin," he said, "no matter what happens." He curled his fingers through her hair and raised his strong arm high, so she was held vertically upward by her very own hair.

Rowen appeared in the door.

"I told you!" Muffin said to Ed. "I told you so. I told you Rowen went to get the police. So there!"

Ed laughed. He twisted her hair until she had to stand right next to him, and he twisted again, forcing her face into the pattern of his shirt.

"Walk outside," said Ed to Rowen.

Muffin said into the shirt, "Row, where are the police?"

"There are no police," said Ed.

At first the hair yanking was just scary, just a weird new pressure, but now it was hurting, and then it was hurting a lot, and it was harder to think about Sam, and harder to keep her balance, and hardest to remember that holding Sam counted the most.

Her big brother said, "Muff and I will take care of Sam for you, Ed. We won't tell anybody anything. Really, Ed. Muff and I are on the same team as you are. We want Dusty's baby to have those great parents. We want the adoption to go through. It's very late and we're all tired and the baby probably needs a bottle, and —"

Ed said, "Get out of the house, kid. Go get your car keys." He began walking Muffin forward. Her feet tangled when he turned her so she was facing forward. Her scalp was higher off her head than it was supposed to be, as if Ed might jerk and peel her scalp away from her skull.

Rowen said, "You don't need this, Ed. A baby and a nine-year-old? They're real pains in the neck. What you need is the money that Cinda and Burt are paying you, and we have to sit down and talk about how we're going to get that."

"Get your keys," said Ed, "or I'll hurt your sister and the baby both."

Then he did jerk hard on her hair, and the thought of her hair coming right off, of Ed standing there with her whole hair in his fist, was so horrific Muffin screamed, which was stupid and wrong, because it frightened her brother. He obeyed Ed. He left the kitchen, which was the last thing Muffin wanted him to do; she felt they must stay with the house until the police got here; and now they were going out into the dark.

Ed marched Muffin over the grass to his car, opened the driver's door, and kneed Muffin into the opening. Ed did not let go of her hair. She didn't see how she could do anything because she had to keep holding Sam.

Rowen raced back, gasping for breath, holding the key chain on one extended finger for Ed to take. Muffin knew what would happen now. Her brother — who liked wrestling and soccer and ice hockey and baseball and tennis — her brother would tackle Ed while Muffin would throw herself sideways into Ed's car with the baby, and scrabble out the other door while they were tussling, and —

"Throw the keys in the woods, Rowen," said Ed. "Your best throw." He changed his grip on her hair, forcing Muffin's head backward until her throat was white and exposed.

"Okay," said Rowen, "okay. Just don't hurt them. Listen to me."

Ed yanked Muffin's head back so far that Muffin screamed with pain as her neck cracked, but there was no scream, because the tilt had flattened her throat out and she could make no sound.

"Throw the keys."

Rowen threw the keys into the woods. It was his best throw. Muffin could hear leaves parting as if for a bullet and she knew they would never find the keys.

"Start backing away from me," said Ed.

Rowen did not move. He said, "Ed, come on, she's only nine."

"I could break her neck," said Ed conversationally.

Rowen backed up.

Muffin hung on to Sam with everything she had. Her brother was getting farther and farther away now. She couldn't see anything but stars, and she was no longer sure whether they were stars in the sky or stars in her brain. She didn't know time, either, and how long Row had been backing.

Ed let go of her hair and shoved her and the baby over on the seat. Then he got in, drove around Row's car and down the drive, accelerating. She and Sam were flung forward, and she twisted hard, trying not to let Sam get bruised, and the hard long curve of the dash smashed into her arm.

She would not cry. She would not cry out, either.

She scootched herself back on the seat, bracing her sneaker bottoms against the dashboard to make herself a stiff safety net for Sam. She had never been in a car without a seat belt. She and Sam bounced and tipped and jarred.

It was an old car, and it smelled of old things, old food and old oil.

Ed picked up his car phone. He tapped in a number.

Muffin buried her face against Sam. He was even littler than she remembered, as if he had shrunk during the day, from not enough food and not enough love and not enough safety.

I am all Sam has, thought Muffin. I cannot make mistakes. This isn't spelling. This isn't arithmetic. This is Sam.

Cinda and Burt had both cars. Neither Cherokee had room for a passenger. They could hardly stand outside in the street shifting boxes and deciding which car to abandon, while Kit yelled for help and the neighbors came with cell phones, guns, and Dobermans.

Cinda and Burt were immobilized at the front door, terrified of leaving the soft sanctuary of the house, equally terrified that Kit's father would have reached the local police and that any second, sirens would come screaming down the road.

Cinda still had her knife, but she had lost track of why she wanted it.

I'd be better off with Cinda, thought Kit. She'll drive, and people driving cars cannot threaten anybody with a knife. She'll have to set it down, maybe next to me where I can use it, or at least on the floor by her feet. She sure can't use it. Cinda's ready to talk. So she's the one I want to be with. I think I can break her down. Or lie to her about Sam, and get her to drive where I want her to drive. And where would that be? What's my master plan now? "Oh, Cinda, would you just turn into that driveway, please, the one marked *Police*?"

"Here," said Kit, taking over. "The best thing to do is find Dusty and talk things through. I'll take the boxes out of Cinda's front seat, and once I've made room —"

"There's room," said Burt. He hauled her toward the navy Jeep as if it had been his idea. "Get on the floor," he ordered. "You can fit."

"Fit" was hardly the word. A tennis ball would have fit in the space on the floor. Kit had to shift boxes and wedge between reams of paper, but she did arrive on the floor of Cinda's Cherokee and Burt did slam the door behind her, while Cinda got in the driver's seat.

Kit found herself starting to giggle. The giggle took hold, and felt good. Down here, hunched over like a dog having kibbles, she could, like a dog, chew on Cinda's ankle if all else failed.

Cinda and Burt were in the midst of a whispered conference when Cinda's car phone rang. Cinda answered it, and the voice that rasped out of the phone was Ed's.

Ed and Dusty. They were still driving around with Sam! Probably looking for Cinda and Burt so they could get the next installment of the adoption payment. So now the three cars would rendezvous — two Grand Cherokees and one ancient Caddy — and money and baby would change hands and Kit would be in the way. And what about that knife?

While Cinda was driving, Kit would just have to get out of the car. Though how she would manage that, scrunched down on all fours, she did not know. She pictured herself opening her door with her toes behind her back, and bumping out fanny first into New Jersey traffic.

"You come and meet me!" said Ed. He was spitting out each syllable. "I want my fifty K! You promised it to me and *I want it*! I already spent some of it. You give me my fifty K! You give it to me *now*. This situation has gotten crazy. Now I've got a damn little kid here, too! You come get this baby, *you bring my fifty thousand*!"

Kit's giggles dried up.

Ed Bing was rabid. He was a mad dog. There would be froth around his mouth.

Cinda spit right back, "We don't have your stupid fifty K," she said in a hot raging whisper.

"Well, I've got the baby; I've got the camera you wanted so much; and I've got the little girl who took the pictures. You bring the fifty K and we're set."

CHAPTER 13

Ed has Muffin, thought Kit.

That's impossible! But where is Rowen? Where is Dusty? How could this have happened?

Muffin with Ed, a mad dog ready to bite.

Cinda got out of the car for the rest of the conversation with Ed, and Kit could not hear what they said to each other, only that Cinda was crying with rage. Then she and Burt had another short conference, Burt kissed the tip of his wife's nose, and they got into their separate cars.

Cinda drove away first, followed by her husband. They drove neatly and carefully, so as not to attract attention. A shiny new sports utility vehicle driven by a woman like Cinda was just right for this neighborhood, though; she belonged. Nobody would notice them.

Ed doesn't want a nine-year-old, thought Kit. He wants cash. He's put himself in a position where he has to have that money. But he's not going to get it. And Muffin and Sam are in his hands.

She remembered those hands. Fat-fingered, swollen, with those heavy, yellow split nails.

Cinda had driven out of Seven Hills. Kit had not seen the knife. If Cinda had it, she'd set it down when Kit was giggling doggy-style. Kit could not base her decisions on a knife that might not be there, that Cinda might not be able to reach.

"Cinda. If you're worried about jail now, what kind of jail is it going to be if Ed has snatched a nine-year-old?"

"He wouldn't do that," said Cinda. Cinda was shaking. Her hands on the wheel, her chin around her mouth . . . her entire body was jittering.

"He has done that. We just heard him say so. He has Muffin." Kit lifted boxes off herself, balancing them on the wide deep dashboard, gripped the armrest, and eased an inch of herself onto the seat. "She's a little girl, Cinda, you met her. She's no wider than a bookmark. And she's somebody else's kid! This is kidnapping, Cinda! Sam — you could maybe talk your way out of that, because some of the time you did have the mother's permission. But you don't have Muffin's mother's permission."

"She'll be fine," said Cinda. The Jeep seemed to drive without her, steadying itself against her unsteady hands.

"We have to call the police, Cinda, so they can go and get Muffin and Sam safely back. You heard Ed's voice. He wants his fifty thousand so much that he is not sane."

Cinda threw her car phone out the window.

Okay, thought Kit, so we won't call the police. She said, "Cinda, how about we go where Ed is waiting and pay him the rest of his money?"

"We don't *have* the fifty thousand," Cinda screamed in fear and fury. "Besides, we paid him the first ten. He's lying. It's forty thousand."

They drove on. Kit wondered where they were going. Did Cinda have a plan? Had she and Burt thought of a place to go, an intelligent thing to do? Were they meeting Ed, with or without the forty or fifty K? Or were they on the run now, shrugging about the fates of Muffin and Sam? "Where is Ed?" asked Kit.

"Forget it. I'm not telling you anything."

Kit located her confessional voice. Her voice that blamed herself. Kit did not often use this voice, but of course she heard it all the time on talk shows. "I've been so stupid today," she said sorrowfully. "It started with Dusty. Dusty never changes. She's stupid all the way through, and even though I know that, today I believed she was different. So I did stupid things. I did a hundred stupid things. And I don't know how come Muffin's older brother isn't with Muffin, but whatever happened makes Rowen stupid, too. Now we have a chance to get smart, Cinda, and we have to take it."

"I am smart!" wailed Cinda. "Don't you bracket me with Dusty! I'm *brilliant.* Burt and I are smarter than anybody. Out in Silicon Valley, in all those new software companies, people are becoming millionaires every day just because they showed up at the right time! And Burt and I are *smarter* than they are, and yet we couldn't get ahead. So we came up with the most brilliant plan." She actually turned toward Kit with a smile. "You see," said Cinda. "Burt and I created a *masterpiece.* I wrote the programs. Very, very sophisticated programming." Cinda nodded with genuine pride. "The way it worked was, and of course I'm simplifying this for you, the stupid customer would stand there getting mad at technology for not giving him his hundred dollars in twenties, and meanwhile, we lift all his bank card information." She was driving easily now, enjoying the tasks of the road: the signaling, lane changing, mirror checking. "We put fake ATMs in six states!" she bragged. "Then Dusty and I would go to real ATMs and take cash out of the accounts."

Kit imagined Cinda's mind exploring once again the programming that had made this scam possible. But Cinda would not refer to it as a scam. Cinda would not admit she was nothing but a purse snatcher, a wallet lifter. Cinda would not picture some poor exhausted woman in her sixties who'd worked all day on her feet at a tough job, and went to the ATM to get cash for groceries — and her account was empty.

You are a common thief, thought Kit.

This was the woman who would have brought up Sam!

Careful not to use the *police* word, Kit said, "But the authorities caught on?"

"Yes! We were so close. Everything was running perfectly. But the other day, we got to our best mall, with the highest traffic, and the police had our ATM staked out." She shook her head. "We spotted them, of course. They're not very smart."

"And the house where we brought the baby — you were leaving it?"

"We looked for that house for so long! It was such a nice house." Cinda seemed pleased by house-hunting memories, like an ordinary woman who'd been comparing kitchens. "It's close to several states. We can hit Pennsylvania, New Jersey, New York, Connecticut, Massachusetts in only a two-hour drive. I even checked the schools in that district, they're excellent, and then Dusty and Ed panicked because we weren't recovering as much cash as we expected to. You should never work with stupid people. They just don't understand that when a business is beginning, there are glitches. We would have paid them eventually."

Kit made noises of sympathy. Cinda and Burt would have had to pay Dusty and Ed eventually, or eventually Dusty and Ed would have turned them in.

Or maybe not!

What was Dusty's role in this?

Kit heard her father's description again: *Dusty's a manipulative woman, extraordinarily selfish.*

If Dusty had been going with Cinda to use the victim's bank cards, Dusty was a common thief, too. Kit thought Dusty would have found it rather entertaining, like shopping; and would have regarded the card owners as no more important than the dolls on her shelf. What mattered was Dusty's space, and Dusty's self.

Dusty had probably treated this as her own delightful *Wheel of Fortune*, without considering that one of these spins, she might lose a turn. Well, they had lost. Big-time.

And Muffin and Sam?

Had they also lost?

How was she going to save them?

Cinda maneuvered through traffic, passing fast and efficiently, darting from lane to lane. Wherever she was going, she was going to get there fast.

Kit felt her way through the arithmetic of Cinda's sophisticated programming. In elementary school Kit had loved word problems, and their little arithmetic people who were real to Kit, and whose lives she used to worry about. (If Josh and Suzette are going to Grandmother's house, and it's 75 miles away, and Josh drives 25 miles an hour and Suzette drives 50 miles an hour, and they both leave at 1:30, when will each child arrive at Grandmother's?) Clearly, Josh was weird. No teenage boy under any circumstance drove 25 miles an hour. No teenage boy would permit his sister Suzette to get there first. Poor Grandmother would have to stand in the door wringing her hands, wondering if Josh had had an accident.

She had to get Cinda bragging again. Had to get Cinda talking again. Every word of information she could glean might help her find out where Ed had Sam and Muffin.

"But Cinda," said Kit, multiplying in her head, "it must have cost a fortune to manufacture a fake ATM so perfect in appearance that nobody questioned it! You had to pay to have it designed and machined and shipped. It must have cost hundreds of thousands of dollars to get the scheme up and going. You must have spent months on it when you weren't earning a salary. And phone lines and I don't even know enough to know what else. Say you already spent two hundred thousand dollars, and you get a hundred each time you steal; you'd have to hit real ATMs with your fake cards *two thousand times* just to get back the money you already spent! If you did ten a day, it would take you two hundred days. And every single time you faked it, you'd be committing a crime and somebody might spot you. Your luck isn't going to hold two thousand times in a row!"

Cinda gave her a junior high school glare; as if Cinda were not thirty, but fourteen. It was eerie to see a kid's sneer on a face twice Kit's age.

I'm telling her she's stupid, thought Kit, when the thing that matters most to Cinda is being smart. "However," said Kit quickly, "I'm sure that once the glitches worked out you would make a fortune. And then you decided you wanted a baby. So you'd have this sweet little family —"

Kit could not keep this up. It wasn't a sweet little family. It was two criminals with a jealousy problem who'd purchased a newborn the way they were purchasing a life — in a shady underhanded way that hadn't worked.

They were at an enormous intersection: many lanes, each with its arrow and an array of gas stations that also sold tacos and doughnuts and charcoal briquettes and had enough pumps for a dozen cars.

Cinda came to a full stop.

I can get out, thought Kit. Walk over to that gas station, where there are ten people there to keep me safe, pick up the phone, and call 911.

But then Cinda and Burt will meet Ed without me, and I won't be there for Muffin and Sam.

Kit could hit Cinda over the head with one of the heavier boxes. Or slam the gear into park and yank out the keys.

But then nobody would go meet Ed.

Ed . . . as desperate for his fifty K as an addict for his needle.

Ed . . . alone with Muffin and Sam.

In the dark of the car, Muffin could not quite see the baby, but he was warm and soft in her arms. He was too quiet, as if he were too tired to cry anymore. Muffin knew instinctively that a baby should never be that tired. A baby should not give up saying how hungry he is.

Sam the Baby was giving up.

He was a very little guy, and he needed more than he was getting.

And Ed on the phone was yelling that he wanted his fifty K.

At first Muffin did not know what K was. In a few sentences she figured out that it was money. "You bring me that fifty K or else!" screamed Ed into the phone.

Or else.

Or else what?

Or else, what happens to Sam and me?

Rowen was running.

He had had to run laps, of course, a jillion times, for warm-ups or for punishment for most teams he'd been on. But running itself did not interest him. Now he ran over potholes, ruts, and piles of gravel and unexpected projecting stones. He ran in complete darkness.

In the distance, a dog howled, and right away another dog howled, closer. A night bird shrieked, and there was a whuffing near his head, and a sort of grunt. The leaves did not rustle, but jostled and clapped. Branches scraped bark.

His running felt so fast that he kept thinking he would catch up to Ed's car. But of course he would never catch up to Ed's car. His little sister, and a stranger's little baby boy, were vanishing.

Had vanished.

His goal was the main road, but once he reached the main road, it wasn't one. Twisting and narrow, it just didn't have traffic. When he'd driven here, he hadn't particularly noticed the pavement itself, but now he saw it had crumbled at the edges, that weeds had worked through cracks. He wasn't going to flag down a rescue because there weren't going to be cars.

His ankle, which he had refused to think about, was throbbing again.

He had to reach the next road, and maybe even the road after that, near Route 80, near that convenience store, and every step he took, no matter how fast he took it, no matter how long his stride, was only the tiniest fraction of what Ed could do.

A car did approach, and Rowen stopped in the road, waving his arms wildly, but the driver leaned on the horn, skidded around him, and never slowed at all.

Row wouldn't have stopped, either, for some strange boy in the road in the middle of the night. Who knew what maniacs were around?

I know what maniacs are around, thought Rowen. And my sister's with one of them.

"There!" said Muffin to Ed. "Stop there. At that store. We have to get Sam milk. He's very very hungry."

The big old Caddy kept right on going. "He stopped crying, that's all I care about," said Ed. Ed's voice was too big. It had swollen, like his hands, like his temper.

"He has to have supper. You have to stop. And diapers, we need diapers. We can't just use a sweater."

Ed looked in her direction. His eyes felt all stare-y, as if they weren't going right. She was glad it was dark and she could not really see him. "It's your cousin, this baby," said Muffin. "Your cousin Dusty had a baby, so this is a numbered cousin. I have some of those. He's your second cousin or your third cousin. I forget how it works. And he needs his milk, your cousin. So you stop the car and buy the milk."

Ed grinned and she saw that he was missing teeth, and she wondered if he would go to the dentist with some of his fifty K, because he looked bad with those gaps in his mouth. "You're a pretty sturdy kid for nine years old," said Ed.

Muffin had been thinking the same thing, and was proud. She *was* a sturdy kid for nine. It wasn't as little as everybody thought. Nine could take care of a baby. Muffin had made a decision not to think about how her head hurt. She had decided to think only about Sam. "Sam is not sturdy," she reminded Ed. "He's all folded over and sickish. He needs his milk."

Ed slowed down, eyeing the store. It

was not the twenty-four-hour store Kit and Muffin had stopped at before. Muffin didn't know where it was. Ed had driven somewhere else completely, which Muffin didn't like, but on the other hand, what difference did it make? She was stuck in the car no matter what. And one good thing, which she knew from training at home and at school and on television, if she could get to a phone — even the one in this car, if Ed would leave her alone — 911 worked anyplace.

Hadn't she said to Rowen and Kit all along that they should call 911?

And had they listened to her?

No. Because she was nine, and nobody listened to nines.

Ed made up his mind. He pulled up in front of the store. It shared a strip with a movie rental place and a dry cleaner. He said, "I'll hold the baby. Here's five dollars."

"I'm not giving you Sam," she said. "You might drive away. You might not take care of him at all. You didn't even bother with a car seat. I have to stay with Sam. You go into the store and buy the milk." I'll use the car phone, she thought. I'll call the police.

"I don't know what to buy," said Ed. He

was laughing at her. "You think I'm gonna leave you with a car phone? You're smart, sister, but you can't outsmart me."

Muffin glared at him. "Then we'll all go in."

"Don't you say a word to anybody," said Ed. "I don't want anybody knowing there's anything happening."

Like people wouldn't wonder why a brand-new baby was blanketed in some old thrown-out sweater. Like people wouldn't wonder why this creepy man and this little girl were showing up at ten-thirty at night with a brand-new baby who ought to be home in his crib. "My door doesn't open," she said.

"I smashed it against your brother's car. Get out on my side."

She sidled over the seats, Sam flopping awkwardly in her arms, and the three of them went inside and put together a baby rescue package. One six-pack of ready-mix formula. One Gerber disposable bottle starter set. One pack of newborn-size Huggies. It was more than five dollars. Ed was mad, but he paid.

On the way back to the car, he put his hand on her shoulder. It didn't hurt, he didn't grip the way he had gripped her hair, and he really didn't do anything. He just put his hand on her shoulder.

But her hair stood up as if he had been yanking on it, and the skin on her arms turned to gooseflesh. She made a pout face to keep herself from gagging. "Sam and I," she said, "will sit in the backseat. It's safer there. The airbag in front might hurt us."

"Yeah, right, like a car this old has airbags," said Ed. "When I get my fifty K, I'll have a car with airbags that could kill you, but not tonight." But he opened the back door, threw the plastic bag of purchases in, and Muffin climbed after it. Ed slammed the door before she was fully inside, not actually catching her left foot in the door, but shoving it in and twisting it.

He laughed and backed roughly out of his parking space, and swung hard and too fast into the road again.

Muffin settled Sam on his back on the seat, leaning over him to hold him safe with her chest while she put together the bottle. Good thing she had had practice. There were several pieces to insert and screw and add. Pouring the formula into the bottle while the car was jouncing around got half of it on her lap. She hadn't washed her hands and she'd touched disgusting things, like this entire car, but she couldn't help that, and she gave the bottle a little squeeze, to get milk on the tip of it, and she brushed the milk on Sam's lips, and tucked the nipple in Sam's mouth, and he began to eat.

It was surprisingly noisy, this baby eating stuff. Sam snurked and snuffled and choked and gulped and hiccuped. But the milk in the bottle disappeared.

Muffin was hungry, too. But she was nine, and strong, and now that she had food for Sam the Baby, so he wouldn't fold up and sicken away, she had to think about *or else*, and how to get them away from it.

"Why do you have that stupid name, anyway?" said Ed from the front seat.

"You mean Sam? Kit picked Sam. It's not a stupid name. It's a strong name, because he's going to be a strong kind of guy."

"I mean Muffin."

"That's not a stupid name."

"Is it your real name?"

"My real name is Margaret." She was not ready to be Margaret. Margaret was the person she would be when she was grown. Margaret was a woman Muffin would meet someday, and recognize.

"*All right*," said Ed suddenly, his voice

completely different. It growled, as if he had turned into a dog; as if she would look over and his face would be fur.

She clung to Sam, as if Sam could save her. As if either of them had any hope.

Nine was not sturdy. Her head hurt, and Sam was heavy, and she was afraid.

"*All right*, here we are," said Ed, parking the Caddy. "And they better have that fifty K. *Or else.*"

CHAPTER 14

Rowen began running again as soon as the car passed him by, running and screaming inside his brain, fear using up the energy he needed to run.

When he heard a second vehicle coming, he went out into the middle of the road and did jumping jacks to signal them.

They stopped.

It was a pickup truck with a double cab. Rifles hung across a rack. Toolboxes lined the truck bed. Two heavyset guys said nothing, but just looked out at him.

Row clutched the triangle of chrome that supported the outside mirror and gasped, "Car phone, you have a car phone? I have to call the police. *My sister.*" He was surprised by the love and the horror in that tiny phrase: my sister. "Somebody took my sister," he said.

* * *

"Where's Burt?" said Cinda. She peered in her rearview mirror and frowned, and then turned in her seat and looked behind her, and then looked way to the right and way to the left. "*Where's Burt?*"

"He's probably back one red light," said Kit, looking around, too.

The light changed, but Cinda did not drive through it.

The car behind them honked instantly and long.

Cinda did not move.

Kit rolled her window down and signaled the car to go around them. It did, the driver shouting obscenities. You don't know how lucky you are, mister, alone in your car and able to go any place you want, Kit thought.

Cinda said, "*Where? Is? Burt?*"

Well, he isn't here, thought Kit. I know where *I'd* be. I'd be on the fastest road out of town.

"If he dumped me . . ." whispered Cinda. Which sounded as if Cinda had been expecting something of the kind.

Is it better or worse that Burt dumped her? Kit thought. How do I field this? I do not care about Cinda's marriage or who goes to prison. I care about Muffin and Sam.

"He probably stopped for a coffee," said Kit lightly. "Or a burger. Probably thought he'd whip into a drive-up window and be out in sixty seconds. Probably he's starving. And then, you know how those things are, he's stuck in a line and they're making some special order for the car ahead of him, and —"

"Shut up!" screamed Cinda.

They waited through another light change.

They were on a commercial stretch where there were several superstores, all closed. The huge empty parking lots were punctuated by lights on silvery poles. A temperature change had turned the air misty, so the light pooled and shimmered in the damp air.

They no longer had a car phone, so they couldn't call Burt to see what was holding him up. Cinda stared at the little pocket that normally held the phone. She fingered it. She said, "What if the police have our license plates? What if they picked him up?"

"We would have seen that," said Kit. "He was behind us a few minutes ago. We'd have seen lights and heard sirens. Wherever he is, he wants to be there."

Cinda stared around the interior of her

car, and examined her hands, and then she even looked at her reflection in her rear-view mirror. "It wasn't supposed to work out like this."

"It hasn't worked out at *all* yet," said Kit. "Here's what we do. We go find Ed. We tell Ed my father is putting together the fifty thousand, which my father can do, he won't even notice it. Then . . ."

Kit had no ideas for *then.*

Then I take Muffin and Sam?

Then Cinda drives away, waving in a friendly fashion?

Then Ed heads home, confident Dad will fly in and hand him fifty thousand dollars?

Cinda whispered, "I will not go to prison. I was not meant for that."

Dusty, too, insisted that things were meant. It was a stupid-person sentence for when you had gotten yourself into a bad corner and you had only yourself to blame and you would not admit it. "I totally agree," said Kit. "You were meant for better things. You write these very sophisticated programs and —"

"Don't patronize me!"

"Fine!" said Kit. "The light has changed six times while we've sat here. So use this so-called brain of yours and do something intelligent. And don't you *dare* hurt the baby boy you wanted to bring up as your own just one hour ago."

The two men hauled Row into their truck.

They were wonderful.

They helped him tell the police what he had to say, they clarified the names of roads and the location of Cinda and Ed's house, they agreed to wait for the cops at the driveway.

They had even just come from McDonald's and handed Rowen the rest of a bag of Chicken McNuggets.

"Ed was going to break my sister's neck. Literally. He was going to take her hair and —"

"He won't do that," said one of the men. "He needs her to hold the baby. He just did that to make you get out of his way."

Hungry as he was, Rowen could not put food in his mouth. He choked; there was no room in his throat. They drove back to the broken white fence and waited for cops. Rowen felt as if he were blacking out, but it was probably exhaustion from the running and fear for Muffin.

When they arrived, the police were patient with him; said how smart he was to have memorized the plate number, color, and make of Ed's car.

But he had not been smart; he'd been dumb all day.

It took no time for the cops to figure out what had been happening in this strange place. One glance at some of the paper on the floor of that abandoned house and the cops knew these were the ATM scammers they'd been trailing. One call and they connected with the cops Kit's father had reached by phone from Seattle. One more call and they connected with cops who'd picked up Dusty Innes sobbing at the side of the road an hour ago. She had wanted to be dropped off at a coffee shop where she insisted her husband would come for her.

Rowen had a harder time connecting. He stalled on the vision of Muffin trapped with Ed — Ed who killed flower beds and cars by running them down; Ed who doubtless entertained himself running down pets in the road.

Ed.

Muffin.

Sam.

"You think you'll get Muffin and Sam pretty quickly?" said Rowen. He had lost control of his voice. It was trembling. The truck driver put an arm on his shoulder and it helped, but not much.

The cops did not fool around with him. Rowen appreciated that. He did not want them to lie to him.

"These two knew we were on to them," said the cop in charge. "We found their fake ATM and we've located a post office drop they use. They'll want to get out of here fast. They've probably got another hideout in some other state. I don't think they're going to want a baby on their hands while they're running, but who knows? Maybe they'll make a deal with Ed Bing on a street corner. But your sister? It's a problem. A newborn can't identify you. A nine-year-old can."

Rowen sagged against the large frames of his rescuers, and they tilted him back upright and stood a little closer to him. He whispered, "But we can all identify them. It's stupid for them to worry about Muffin when there's also Kit and me to worry about."

"Right," agreed the cop. "But, see, everybody in this is stupid. You don't know what stupid people are going to do when they get cornered. A computer thief, now: He's really proud of his sophisticated programming. That's their favorite word —*sophisticated.* Your computer hacker thinks all the time how he's smarter than anybody. You corner him and now he has to admit he's as stupid as the next jerk and he doesn't want to admit that. And that makes him dangerous. Smart people think they shouldn't have to pay a price the way crummy old burglars do. Smart people think they should get bonus points for committing a crime. They didn't work prison into their equation. They had fun figuring out a system where they'd never get caught, and now they're caught, and they're terrified because prison is out there. Years of prison, just as horrible and disgusting and scary as it is for anybody who ever stole a car or dealt drugs. And now, even if nobody meant it to happen, they've kidnapped two children, and they know it, even if they're pretending not to know it. So they're scared, kid. Everybody in this is not just stupid. Everybody in this is dangerous."

In their navy Cherokee, among their boxes, Cinda and Kit sat while the traffic screamed at them and circled them.

"Get out of the car," said Cinda.

"Why?" said Kit. "Where are you going?"

"I'm not going to tell you that. Now *get out of the car.*"

Great, thought Kit. Now I'm going to be stranded on the side of a road, with no idea where Ed is, and no idea where Muffin and Sam are, while Cinda disappears, and I won't even know where *she* is. In fact, I don't even know where *I* am. I can call 911 at last, but I won't have a clue to give them. "Is your last name really Chance?"

"Don't be ridiculous. Chance is a joke."

"It's not a joke. It caught you in the end. You can't gamble as much as this, Cinda, and not lose eventually."

"Get out of the car."

"No. I won't. You drive me to where Ed is supposed to meet you, and then I'll get out of the car."

Cinda began to cry again. "The man I love just drove away and doesn't care what happens to me," she whimpered.

"Well, don't look at me for sympathy!" yelled Kit. "You're a mean selfish stupid lowlife who won't even drive across the street to help out the baby you were going to adopt. Drive off a bridge, see if I care!"

"Not a bad idea," said Cinda. Her tears

were instantly gone, as if her emotions had faucets. She snickered. Her features settled themselves in creepy animal ways, as if she had turned feral.

Their light was red, but she paid no attention to it, or to the traffic that had the green.

She put her foot on the gas and accelerated, and her crazed laugh filled the car like dollars floating out of a cash machine.

She's going to kill us, thought Kit.

She'd rather crush herself against a cement wall than go to trial and be proved stupid.

And I'm in the same car.

Muffin sat tight.

She pulled her tummy in and tucked her elbows around Sam. She tried to be the tiniest package there was. She looked out once, and could not look out again.

Ed had parked the car. He had gotten out of it, slamming his door so hard that the car actually rocked. He was so angry that Muffin thought he might try to tip the car over, and she and Sam would fall on their heads. Because fifteen minutes had gone by, and Cinda and Burt were not here with the fifty K.

Or else was getting closer and closer.

They were not in a rescue place.

In her one look out the window, she'd seen nothing but a mean and scary night. The mist seemed thick and hot, as if it would burn. The night roared, like monsters, and even trembled, like a volcano preparing to erupt, while Ed circled the car, stomping at each corner of the car and smacking the hood or the trunk with his fist. Ed smoked one cigarette after another, sucking them down like Sam with his bottle, except Ed was not satisfied, and halfway through one cigarette would hurl it into the air and start the next, ripping a match down as if decapitating something.

They were alone in this terrible hot light place with its wet air and trembling earth.

Even though Cinda and Burt were not good guys, they weren't as bad bad guys as Ed was. And Muffin had thought that she and Sam would go with Cinda and Burt, and somehow it would be okay.

But Cinda and Burt were not coming.

And Ed knew it, and he was stomping the bottoms of his feet into the asphalt, because he could do nothing but wait.

How long would Ed wait?

How long before *or else*?

Down on her lap, inside his tiny world, a tiny boy finished his supper.

He finished baby-fashion, falling asleep, so the nipple fell out of his mouth and the last of the milk ran down his cheek and soaked into the old sweater.

Muffin had nothing to wipe his cheek with.

Babies were supposed to have little shirts. And little teeny sneakers with little teeny Velcros. And little teeny bib blue jeans, like miniature farmers. Babies were supposed to have their grandmothers around, and the neighbors, and baby powder on the shelf. Babies were supposed to be sung to, and rocked, and have special wallpaper on the wall.

Sam didn't know that.

He didn't know a single thing yet.

But Muffin knew, and what's more, Dusty knew. Ed knew. Cinda and Burt knew. They all knew.

And they didn't do it.

They let Sam be a baby and they didn't treat him like one. They threw him around like the six-pack of milk Ed had thrown into the backseat.

And Muffin knew then that the mommy can't waste time being scared. The mommy has to take care of things. And there was only one mommy around.

Muffin.

Cinda found the bridge quickly.

It was not the kind of bridge she could drive off. It was the kind of bridge she could drive into. Arching, soaring cement supports lifted another highway over the one Cinda drove on. Cinda had reached seventy-five miles an hour. She aimed for the bridge and Kit could do nothing except cringe behind her seat belt and hope the airbag took care of her. At this speed, she doubted anything could take care of her. She had been too stupid all day to waste the Lord's time praying for her own safety. In the split second left to her, she prayed for the safety of Sam and Muffin.

But Cinda was a coward.

She took her foot off the gas.

She continued to steer, the Cherokee lost velocity, Kit took the rim of the steering wheel, and said loudly, "Pull over, Cinda. Stop the car."

Cinda obeyed.

Kit took the keys out of the ignition.

The doors on the right side of the big old Cadillac did not open, because of the dents

Ed had put into it, so Muffin and Sam had to get out the door on the left side, where Ed was stomping. She slid her feet out first and thunked herself and Sam onto the pavement.

Ed stormed over. "Where do you think you're going?"

She put Sam on her shoulder. For a lightweight guy, he could get very heavy, very quick. "We're getting fresh air."

He snorted. "There's a truck stop right over there. Fifty semis idling. There's no fresh air in this entire state."

She turned, and now that she was on the outside of the terrible old car and was standing up, she could see the trucks. It was their engines making the roar; their engines making the ground tremble, making the night hot.

It was just trucks, and she had thought it was volcanoes.

Through the mist she could see the shapes of drivers coming and going from their trucks. The drivers were grown-ups. The drivers, thought Muffin Mason, would be daddies.

I'm here, she thought. I need you. Sam needs you. Come get us!

"Get back in the car," said Ed roughly.

The truck stop was across the road.

The road had eight lanes.

She was marooned here with Ed as if ocean currents and sharks cut her off.

And fathers, daddies, were right there — within sight — to make things fine for Sam, and they didn't know. They'd come if they knew.

Kit Innes was grateful for other people's car phones.

No fewer than three drivers had telephoned in the description of Cinda and her license plate and suicidal driving. A police car arrived so fast that Kit didn't even have to come up with a plan for how to reach them.

The officer was gentle with Cinda. Polite. Complimentary. He told her how smart she was, how sophisticated her programming had been, how she had kept agents in several states wracking their brains.

Kit would have vomited if she had to say that many nice things to Cinda.

The officer agreed with Cinda that it was terrible how Burt had abandoned her, a gentleman would not do that, Cinda had been meant for better things, Cinda with her extraordinary cleverness.

He said, "And where were you supposed

to meet Ed? Where did Ed take Muffin and Sam?"

"You can't blame that on me. I didn't have a single thing to do with Ed snatching that nine-year-old. That's his problem."

"But it is a kind of big problem, Cinda," said the policeman in a warm, affectionate voice. "Because after all, we have a newborn and a nine-year-old with a dangerous guy, a guy who might hurt them, and you can help. That's a good thing for you to do. Because you're in sort of a crummy situation here, you know, and helping would be a good thing to do."

Cinda could no longer be swept up by the thought of her large brain. Her power to rob was gone. Her power to impress others was gone. But she had one power left. And she was keeping that power.

Cinda smirked at the officer. "I'm not telling," said Cinda.

Chapter 15

In school last year, when Muffin had been in third grade (a grade Rowen said didn't even count as school, you didn't learn anything real in third grade), they had learned about the *Titanic*.

A huge ship that sank years and years ago. Before her grandparents had been born. There were many many people on the ship, and most of them did not live, because there were not enough lifeboats. They sank in the icy icy North Atlantic. But that terrible night, when the *Titanic* went down, something had been done for the first time ever.

It didn't help the *Titanic*.

It might help Muffin and Sam.

I did so learn something, Rowen, she thought. And I remember it, too. So there.

"Sam and I are sitting in the front seat,"

she said to Ed, holding her chin high. "We'll listen to the radio."

Ed opened the door for them, and Muffin's teeth hurt from the squeal of the hinges. Ed took the car phone and fastened it to his belt loop. He laughed at her, to prove that he had known what she was up to.

Well, he had not known.

"Don't turn on the radio," he said. "Stupid car like this, it would run the battery down. You wait till I get my fifty K, *then* I'll have a decent car." He slammed the door on them, keeping the phone, but leaving the keys in the ignition, and then he sat on the car itself, he sat on the trunk, facing away from Muffin. He studied the roads, to watch who came. Even if he never looked back at Muffin, she and Sam could not sneak out of the car. The door would scream.

Muffin sturdied herself. She was nine. Nine was old enough to figure things out. Muffin studied the dashboard. She studied the wheel. She studied every button, arm, and lever.

She was too young to have thought much about driving, and she had never thought about this particular aspect of driving. But if you turned the ignition partway, the engine would not run, and no sound would give you away to Ed sitting on the car, but the battery would make power.

You could use the headlights.

Across the sea of eight lanes of highway, in the huge truck stop parking lot, were four fathers. They had never met. They didn't care about one another. They didn't know one another's names. They didn't drive for the same company. All they did was come out of the cafeteria at the same time and head toward their trucks.

Across that sea of highway, through the misty night, they could see a single car parked alone in an empty lot that by day would be filled with thousands of cars. It was too foggy to make out details. But in the fog, the light from the parked car's headlights expanded, shivered, and hung in the night air.

Three short blips of light.

Three long blips of light.

Three short blips of light.

And then dark.

One trucker shrugged. "Kids," he said, and got in his truck and drove away.

One trucker said, "Some woman with a flat. I'm not changing it for her. They want equality, let 'em change their own tires." He drove away.

The third trucker said, "Let's check it out. I've never seen an SOS before."

"Yeah, we'll walk over," said the fourth trucker. "Be a pain to drive." He opened the door to his own cab and his German shepherd leaped out. It was a huge beautiful dog.

"Your dog safe?" asked the third trucker. The two men headed for the eight-lane highway. Not much traffic. They might have to pick up the pace a little, but they'd run across without trouble.

"Nope. She's basically pretty mean."

"You use a leash?"

"Nope. Defeats the purpose."

They were both laughing as they walked toward the beat-up old sedan. When they got close, they could make out a skinny guy sitting on the trunk, smoking.

The guy was shocked to see them come straight toward him, and he jumped down to the pavement and saw the dog, and saw how the fur on the dog's shoulders and neck was standing up, and saw that there was no leash, and he got back up on the trunk.

"You rang?" said one trucker to the skinny guy.

"What are you talking about? What are you doing here? Leave me alone. Get out of here!" The guy looked around the parking lot in a frenzied way, but nothing had changed in the parking lot except that the two truckers and the dog had arrived, and all of a sudden the guy put out his cigarette, grinding it down into the hood of his own car like he was killing something, and he began swearing, and screaming about his fifty K, and the truckers thought it must be a drug deal they'd interrupted, and inside the car, huddled against the far passenger door, they saw the little kid with her doll.

"There's our SOS," said the dog owner.

The skinny guy vaulted off the hood, yelling what he was going to do to the little girl.

The truckers were not slow. They were used to stupid little cars burping in front of them. They were used to deer crossings and hitchhikers standing too far out in the driving lane.

"Get 'im, Jaws," said the dog's owner, which Jaws did, because Jaws liked doing that, and the other trucker opened the car door and picked up a little girl who was not, after all, holding a doll.

* * *

By the middle of the night, at the police station there were enough parents to go around.

Muffin's mother and father hugged her constantly, crying, "Our poor little girl! Our poor baby!" until Muffin was thoroughly annoyed. She had not been a poor little girl. She had made the right decisions and handled things well, especially Sam the Baby and the very first SOS from a superstore parking lot in New Jersey.

It just kept on being true. When you were nine, they didn't give you credit.

Aunt Karen and Uncle Anthony and Shea arrived with armloads of baby gear, because Aunt Karen had meant to pack Shea's baby things for fifteen years now, and had only gotten the boxes as far as the fourth step of the attic stairs, so she had easy access to all the blankets and terry jumpsuits Sam the Baby might need.

Shea rushed over to Kit. She seemed a total stranger to Kit: The people Kit knew were Rowen and Muffin and Sam. "How could you leave me out of this?" cried Shea. "Why didn't you call? I would have loved this! I was watching movies and feeding gerbils while you were having car chases! No fair."

Kit's mother and stepfather alternately

hugged her and yelled at her. "Why didn't you tell me when I phoned your father's house?" demanded her mother. "Why didn't you tell me you had this baby there? I would have come straight over! None of this would have happened! It was — so —"

"Stupid," agreed Kit, who had had time to consider brains. "You're right. I was stupid."

She felt that Shea wanted to get into this discussion, and motioned her to stay silent.

"Nothing got you out of this nightmare except pure good luck, Kit," said Malcolm.

Muffin narrowed her eyes at Kit's stepfather. "*I* got Sam and me out of it," she said pointedly.

Rowen stood on the sidelines. He had played a lot of games as star this and best that and most valuable something else. He had never expected to be on the bench when the real action occurred. He had certainly not anticipated that his baby sister would be smarter than he was.

Shea came over to sit with him and he told her nothing. He would someday, but he was wrung out with all the things he had done wrong.

Kit's father called from his plane. He didn't have enough details to be able to call his daughter stupid; he didn't know about that yet; so he mainly called Dusty stupid. Just before he hung up, he said to Kit, "No matter what, don't let anybody pretend Dusty has come to her senses. She doesn't have any."

The police had gone back to the coffee shop where they'd deposited Dusty after her most recent set of lies. So probably the most important parent at the police station that night was Dusty herself.

The only known parent of Sam the Baby.

But when Dusty tried to pick Sam up, Muffin reacted like Jaws the dog. "Don't you let her touch Sam!" said Muffin loudly to the assortment of police and parents. "She is a bad, mean woman."

"I am not! I'm never mean!" Dusty was hurt. "I've made mistakes. But I've learned. And I'm going to give this a try."

"You're saying that only because there are witnesses," said Kit. "You want to look good. Well, you can't. There's no way you can look good again. You were selling your son, the price was right. And you knew all along, you knew for months, what kind of people Burt and Cinda are. You helped them with their ATM nonsense. So don't tell me you'll *try* to be a parent. Muffin's right. You shouldn't even touch Sam."

"I'm going to work on it," said Dusty, lifting her chin to look brave.

"He's not an it," said Kit. "He's a little guy who needs all the attention all the time."

Dusty got belligerent. She glared at her former stepdaughter. "It isn't your decision, Kit Innes."

"It isn't yours, either," said a policewoman. "The baby will be taken care of by social services while we sort things out. You have not yet been charged, Mrs. Innes, but Cinda has stated that you were the one who drove from ATM to ATM using the fake cards to get cash."

"I was not!" cried Dusty. "They're lying! They're just trying to spread the blame!" Dusty was shocked to be led where Cinda had been taken before her: deep inside the police station. As if she had done something wrong. "I wasn't meant for this," she said in a high strangled voice. "This wasn't supposed to happen!" She looked back at Kit, as if expecting Kit to prevent this.

The door closed after Dusty.

Burt was still on the road somewhere, still hoping to get away, still hoping to prove himself smarter than the cops.

The social worker arrived with a car carrier; the right kind; the big fat plastic white kind, in which babies lay safely. Aunt Karen had dressed Sam in a sweet little terrycloth suit, with embroidered balloons and a matching blanket.

What if I never know what happens to Sam? thought Kit, and her heart lurched.

What if Sam the Baby had been in her life only twelve hours, and would never be in her life again?

"We can't keep him?" whispered Muffin.

"No," said the social worker gently. "You were a very brave, very fine friend for Sam. You were the best he could ever have. But somebody else is going to decide who Sam's mommy and daddy should be."

"I don't want you to take him away," wailed Muffin. "How do we know you're choosing the right people to take care of him?"

We don't know, thought Kit. Her hair prickled. Her eyes filled. *And we won't know.*

Sam slept without knowing anything of his world. He just slept. He was entirely sleep. And he was going out into the world by himself, just another child in the terrifying lottery of parents.

I won the parent lottery, thought Kit. Rowen and Muffin did, too. Shea did.

Kit loved all three of them fiercely. She

loved Muffin for her bravery, her refusal to give up, her brains. She loved Rowen for running, for trying, for succeeding. She loved Shea for being jealous of their adventure, when it had not been an adventure; it had been a hell.

She wanted good parents and good friends for Sam the Baby.

Oh, Sam! she thought. Please, Lord, watch over Sam. He needs You.

She kissed Sam good-bye. She pressed her cheek on his soft perfect face. Sam didn't know. He wouldn't recognize her if he saw her again. "Be careful for him," Kit said to the social worker. "Find somebody to love him."

"I promise," she said, and then Sam was gone from their lives, and the parents and the children who were left clung to one another.

About the Author

Caroline B. Cooney lives in a small seacoast village in Connecticut. She writes every day on a word processor and then goes for a long walk down the beach to figure out what she's going to write the following day. She's written over fifty books for young people, including, *The Party's Over*; the acclaimed *The Face on the Milk Carton* Trilogy; *Flight #116 Is Down*, which won the 1994 Golden Sower Award for Young Adults, the 1995 Rebecca Caudill Young Readers' Book Award, and was selected as an ALA Recommended Book for the Reluctant Young Adult Reader; *Flash Fire*; *Emergency Room*; *The Stranger*; and *Twins*. *Wanted* and *The Terrorist* were both 1998 ALA Quick Picks for Reluctant Young Adult Readers.

Ms. Cooney reads as much as possible, and has three grown children.